"Why don't I come over to see you?" Darren whispered. "You can show me around."

"I don't know, Darren. I should ask the Holdens first."

"Ask them if it's okay when you get there." His lips brushed my cheek and nuzzled my neck.

I couldn't think. "Okay," I answered.

"I should meet my competition, shouldn't I?"

"Your competition?" Jon Prince's image suddenly flashed into my head.

"Sammy . . . the chimp." Darren kissed my neck again. "Who else is there?"

"No one, and you know it," I answered quickly. "No one at all."

Caprice Romances from Tempo Books

A CAPRICE ROMANCE

Wanted: A Little Love
Stephanie Gordon Tessler

TEMPO BOOKS, NEW YORK

WANTED: A LITTLE LOVE

A Tempo Book / published by arrangement with
the author

PRINTING HISTORY
Tempo Original / September 1984

ISBN: 0-441-87169-0

Tempo Books are published by The Berkley Publishing Group,
200 Madison Avenue, New York, New York 10016.
Tempo Books are registered in the United States Patent Office.
PRINTED IN THE UNITED STATES OF AMERICA

TO MY FAVORITE MOM

*Who always loved me
even when I was a little monkey*

TO MY FAVORITE CHILDREN

*Whom I'll always love
even when they're little monkeys
just like their mom*

Chapter One

WANTED: reliable young person to baby-sit.
Some evenings/weekends. Must love animals.
Must be patient and loving. $5.00 an hour. Call
Holden Ranch—555-4343.

Up. Down. Up. Down. Pedaling my bicycle for so long was making me hot and sweaty. "I'll never make it," I panted. "Five dollars an hour. Five dollars an hour," I reminded myself. "You'll make it, Freddie Larson—or else."

Either the Holden Ranch was not as close by bicycle as it had sounded over the phone, or I was in much worse shape than I'd thought. I had at least a mile to go before I reached Old Canyon Road and I was already exhausted. This was the first time I'd actually ridden my bike out this far. When we first moved to Southern California, Mom, Dad, and I often went for drives and toured around the San Fernando Valley. The rural areas we liked to call the great western outback had always seemed a lot closer—by car.

1

I pushed my sunglasses back up my slippery nose, as sweat trickled out of my hair and down my face. If I didn't arrive at the Holden place soon, I'd need another bath.

"Hi, I'm Sweaty Freddie," I could announce. Some great first impression that ought to make.

And I was counting on impressing the Holdens right off the bat. As much as I despised baby-sitting, at five dollars an hour this was a job I wanted. More than wanted—needed.

There was no way Darren Gresham was going to Winter-fest without me. When the senior class of Woodlake High School arrived in Mammouth Mountain to spend two glorious weeks of winter vacation in the snow, I intended to be right there with them.

To do that, I needed three hundred dollars. A five-dollar-an-hour job was a real find. But why someone would pay that much for a baby-sitter was beyond me. The way I figured it, the Holdens had to have at least a dozen kids, each and every one of them an absolute monster. That's why their ad had specified someone who liked animals. They meant wild animals. The Holden household was probably a zoo. I'd bet their kids were . . . But then, I reminded myself, what difference did it make to me what they were? I was desperate and I had to take the job—no matter what.

"I'll even baby-sit a boa constrictor for five bucks an hour," I admitted candidly. I knew I didn't have a whole lot of alternatives.

There was a sign at the entrance to the Holdens. It wasn't the type of impressive gateway you'd expect to see at a ranch—not the kind of spread John Wayne owned in all his westerns. The sign read HOLDEN'S FUNNY FARM. Not very reassuring.

The gate was open so I pushed my bike through. I was trying to decide if I should shut the gate behind me, when an old battered pickup truck whizzed past me stirring up the roadway and showering me **with choking** clouds of dust.

"Thanks a lot, you creep!" I **shouted** as the truck sped away. I tried to see who the **big ape behind the** wheel was, but I couldn't make him out; he **looked like a man** in a cowboy hat.

I examined my red knit shirt **and jeans**. "Drat. That's just what I needed, a dirt bath." A sudden thought occurred to me. What if the driver had been Mr. Holden? I hoped he hadn't seen me shaking my fist at him as he drove away.

The long road up to the house was unpaved and dusty and full of ruts, but it was lined by lovely old willows that crossed branches high overhead and covered me with welcome green shade. It was a really beautiful ride under the trees, and it gave me a chance to cool down before I met the Holdens and their brood.

The house was reassuring, a pretty one-story with yellow siding and white trim. There were plenty of flowers and trees around it. A vine with little purple flowers grew over the trellises and onto the roof of the porch.

"Kind of charming," I muttered. "But it's so quiet." Too quiet for a ranch with livestock and things. I listened for a moo or a cluck. Not even a dog barked. Where were all the wild animals I was expected to love?

I kicked down my bike stand and slowly went up the stairs to the porch. So this is Holden's Funny Farm, I thought, looking around. Just how appropriate was that name? At the front door I ran my fingers through my hair, brushed the dust off my jeans, then knocked.

"Tall, blond, a smattering of freckles across your nose. . . . Exactly how I pictured you. You must be Fredrika," announced the thin man who opened the door.

"Me? Oh . . . yes, I am. Fredrika Larson." No one called me Fredrika except my grandma Sylvia. I stuck out my hand and we shook. Keep it firm, I reminded myself. Dad says people respect you if you have a good firm grip.

"I'm Noah Holden, Fredrika. Come in." Mr. Holden seemed tall to me as I stepped past him into the entry.

"Is that her?" called a woman from the back of the house.

"It's her, Birdie," the man answered.

"Oh, good. I'm on my way."

Noah Holden led the way into a room with a great stone fireplace and lots of big, comfortable-looking furniture. "This is the den, and family room, and playroom, and TV room. In other words, if we aren't eating or sleeping, we are always in here."

"It's nice. Very cozy." I didn't know what I was expected to say.

"Cozy and battered, but it's comfortable. With our kid, you need a place that can take a beating. We save the living room for company."

Our kid? Or did he say kids? The furniture did look a little climbed on. "Oh, sure. That's what my mom does, too. I haven't seen the living room since I was six."

Mr. Holden laughed. "I like you, Fredrika."

"Please call me Freddie, Mr. Holden. Everybody does."

"Okay, Freddie. And you can call me Noah. . . ."

"And I'm Birdie, Freddie. Short for Roberta, which I detest." Birdie Holden bounded into the room.

Noah and Birdie were a study in contrasts. He was tall and thin with straight dark hair. His lean tanned face had deep laugh lines that were white against his dark skin when he wasn't smiling. He laughed and smiled a lot.

Birdie wasn't small, just short compared to Noah. She was round and cute. Her face was a glowing sun, covered with freckles and surrounded by a halo of bouncy red curls. They looked good together—different, yet compatible.

Birdie pumped my hand vigorously and smiled broadly. She made me feel welcome and a little more at ease. I already

liked the Holdens. Silently, I prayed they were getting the
same good vibes from me.

"Sit down, Freddie. So we can talk," Birdie suggested.
We sat side by side on the worn brown couch. "Tell us
something about yourself. You must like kids and animals, or
you wouldn't have answered our ad. Do you live near here?
What made you decide to take this job? Do you—"

"Whoa, Birdie. Give her a chance." Noah got up from the
arm of the couch where he'd perched behind his wife.
"Look. I'll get us some sodas, okay? And you take it easy on
the poor kid while I'm gone."

"That's all right. I don't mind," I assured him.

"Sorry. I guess I am a little overanxious. This is the first
time I've ever had to hire a sitter for Sammy. One of us has
always been home with him. I'm a little uptight," Birdie
admitted.

"Me too. I've done a lot of sitting for my aunt. I have a
little cousin who's four. And I've sat for several of our
neighbors' kids. But I always knew them and their parents.
This is my first baby-sitting job for people I don't know. If I
get the job, that is."

"Have you ever done any other kind of work?" Noah
asked, returning with a tray of soft drinks and putting them
down on the coffee table in front of us. "Is this your first
interview? We know how awful interviews can be, don't we,
honey?"

Birdie smiled up at Noah and nodded her head.

"I did have one other interview, once. But I don't think it
counts. I used to volunteer, with some of my friends, as a
candy striper at the Children's Hospital. But they needed
people so badly, I think they would have taken me if I'd been
a trained gorilla."

Birdie and Noah looked at each other and laughed.

"Why did you quit?" asked Noah.

I knew that question was coming. I was afraid that my answer would make me look bad. Still, I couldn't lie. "I really didn't like working in the hospital. I loved all the kids—maybe too much. It depressed me to see so many of them so sick. Sometimes we played with the kids or read them stories, but candy stripers usually just do busywork and run errands. We couldn't give the sick kids what they needed most—their health. I felt helpless because I couldn't do anything for them. I think the kids sensed I didn't belong there. I know my supervisor did. I only lasted three months. Only one of my friends, Barbara, really liked it. She still works there."

I stared down at the toe of my running shoe. It was embarrassing to admit that I'd failed miserably as a candy striper. I wondered if the Holdens would consider my failure a flaw in my character? I'd pictured myself as an angel of mercy, all in white, when my friends and I had decided to volunteer. I'd turned out to be a flower arranger in a peppermint-stick uniform. When Sandi and Janet had decided volunteering was a waste and quit, I'd quit with them. Even now, I felt as if I'd let someone down—maybe myself.

"You're awfully hard on yourself for not becoming the world's greatest hospital volunteer. You liked the children, right? That's what counts. Not everyone is cut out to work with sick people." Birdie took my hand and patted it gently.

These were nice people. Suddenly I didn't care if their Sammy had two heads and a tail. If I had to baby-sit, I wanted to work for them.

"I guess I would've had to quit the hospital eventually, anyway. I didn't get paid for volunteering. I answered your ad because I need to earn some money."

"A car?" Noah guessed. "Teenagers always want wheels."

"No. Not a car. I really don't need one. I get to use our old station wagon if my parents don't need it. My high school class is planning a trip to the mountains for two weeks in December. We're going to raise most of the money by class projects. But we'll each need three hundred dollars extra. I want to earn the money to pay my share myself."

"Admirable endeavor, I'd say." Noah nodded his head in approval and handed me a glass of soda. "Did Birdie explain anything about our work? Why we have to leave Sammy alone?"

Since I had a mouthful of cola bubbles and couldn't answer, I just shook my head.

"We're in the industry," Noah continued. "Entertainment, that is. Movies. TV. Usually one of us works and the other one is home minding the ranch."

"And Sammy," Birdie interjected.

"And Sammy. But we've been offered the most important job we've ever had." Noah looked genuinely pleased.

"It's going to take both of us to do the handling on the set, and that means leaving Sammy." Concern clouded Birdie's eyes. Then she smiled at Noah. "There is a good side. Because it's a public location, the university campus, we'll only have to work one evening during the week—mostly Friday nights—and Saturdays and Sundays; that's when the area is closed to the public."

"What do you think?" asked Noah.

They both looked at me. "I think . . . that's . . . great?"

"No. What do you think about the hours? Can you handle it with your school schedule?" he asked.

"Do you want the job?" Birdie looked at me hopefully.

Did I want it? "Yes. Oh, yes. I can handle it. It'll be perfect. I do want the job. Thank you."

"Except . . ." Birdie hesitated.

She had doubts about me. I knew it. She thought I wasn't responsible enough because I'd quit the volunteer job. "Except?" I repeated.

"Except, before you say yes, I think you should meet Sammy. To see if you two hit it off." Birdie got up from the couch and led the way down the hall toward the back of the house.

The moment of truth was upon me. It didn't matter if I liked Sammy or not. If he didn't like me, it was all over. It was obvious that the Holdens adored their son. I just knew they loved him more than anything else in the whole world—and they spoiled him terribly. I had a feeling about Noah and Birdie's little boy. Their little Sammy was going to be a handful.

"No matter what, kid, you're going to love me," I whispered under my breath. "I'm ready for you, Sammy Holden. I'm ready for anything."

"He's up," Birdie squealed gaily, stepping into the room in front of me. "There he is, my precious baby."

I stood between the Holdens, Noah on one side, Birdie on the other, staring at the crib in the middle of the room. In the crib stood Sammy, chattering to us happily, his arms outstretched in welcome. My head reeled, my knees shook, I blinked my eyes. This I wasn't ready for. Silently, I demanded my mouth to smile and my knees to hold me up.

Sammy Holden was a *chimpanzee*!

Birdie lifted her "precious baby" from the crib, hugging him close and crooning sweet things in his ear. She looked at Noah and me and smiled. Noah returned her smile proudly. To Noah and Birdie, Sammy, dressed in diapers, all furry arms and legs, was like a real child.

How do you baby-sit a chimp? How do you make it like you? How do you feed it? How do you dress it? How do you change it? I didn't have time to worry about the other two thousand questions that zoomed through my head.

Birdie held Sammy out to me.

I raised my arms slowly. I couldn't move forward. I stared at the huge teeth and puckered lips moving toward me. For the first time in my life, a real live monkey put his arms around my neck, squeezed me in a hairy embrace, and planted a wet and noisy raspberry on my cheek. I closed my eyes and swallowed hard.

Five dollars an hour. Five dollars an hour, I repeated over and over inside my head. For five dollars an hour, I hugged Sammy back.

Chapter Two

"ALL RIGHT!" NOAH CHEERED. "You've passed the hardest part of the test. Hasn't she, Birdie?"

Birdie grinned happily. "Sammy likes you, Freddie. And I like you. And Noah likes you, too. Don't you, dear?"

"You bet I do. I know Freddie and Sammy are going to get along great. Now we can work Tiger with clear minds. If we don't have to worry about Sammy, we can give our complete attention to handling him."

"A chimpanzee? And a tiger? Are you animal trainers in a circus? I thought you were actors in the movies and on TV." A tiger in the house, too. I started to shake.

"Whoops." Birdie giggled. "We forgot to tell you exactly what it is we do in the industry."

"We raise and train wild animals, Freddie. For movies, TV, commercials, whenever an animal is needed," explained Noah. "The animal compound is about half a mile from the house."

"We trained Taurus, the root-beer bull. Do you remember the ads where he crashes down the wall every time someone says the name of the root beer?" asked Birdie.

"And Clyde, the lion who wanders around New York and advertises raincoats. You've seen him, haven't you? And the goat that sold deodorant? That was us. Well, actually it was Woodrow Wilson, but we trained him. You've probably seen a lot of our work," said Noah.

I tried to ignore Sammy, who was busy inspecting my hair for nonexistent bugs. "Sure I have. I know all those ads. Is that what you're going to be working on now? More commercials? With a tiger?" I shifted Sammy to my other hip. He began to poke at one of the golden heart earrings I wore.

"Here. Let me," offered Noah. He took Sammy from me and began to walk back to the family room.

"It's much better than a commercial," he said, sitting down on the braided rug and pulling Sammy into his lap. "We did a pilot for a television show that aired during the summer. It's been picked up for syndication by a major network."

"What does that mean?"

"A pilot is an introductory show for a weekly series. Going into syndication means it's been bought by a TV station. We start filming next week," said Birdie.

"Has the pilot been on TV? Have I seen it?" It was exciting to think I knew someone who was actually going to be on TV every week. Or at least their tiger would.

"You might have." Sammy was busy sucking on the buttons of Noah's sport shirt. Noah moved the chimp to his other knee to distract him. "It's about this college kid who hatches an egg as an experiment in his biology class. And it turns out to be a duck, who gets bonded to him and thinks the student is its mother."

"That's *Duck Donald*! I saw it. I loved it, too." Suddenly I understood. Tiger wasn't a tiger; he was a trained duck. I sighed with relief.

My enthusiasm caught Sammy's attention. He waddled over to me and climbed up into my lap. He smelled awful.

"Phew, Sammy. You need a change," Birdie noted, wrinkling her nose.

Steady, Freddie, I warned myself, getting another whiff of Sammy.

"How about it, Freddie? Ready to begin your lessons on taking care of my little sweetie here?"

Sweetie? The way he smelled? Birdie had to be kidding.

"Oh sure." I sounded brave, but I doubted I'd ever be that ready. "Ready Freddie, that's me," I announced loudly, following Birdie back to Sammy's bedroom.

I could hardly believe I'd actually done it. I had the job. I was going to be rich. I'd be able to earn the three hundred dollars for Winterfest by working Friday nights and weekends. Mom and Dad were going to be so proud of me when they heard. But Darren was going to be furious. I'd be working almost every weekend until Christmas vacation.

The station wagon was in the garage when I parked my bike. That meant my parents were home. I raced into the kitchen through the door from the garage. I was so anxious to share my news, I didn't see Dad standing in front of the stove and practically ran into him.

"My turn to cook. I thought I'd try something different tonight. How does curried armadillo sound, Fred?"

"Gross, Dad. It'll probably taste like salad, lamb chops, mashed potatoes, and spinach."

"Probably. I don't think it's smart to mess around with perfection. Lamb chops I'm good at." His blue eyes sparkled at me from under heavy grayish-brown brows.

"But lamb chops every third night . . . Boring, Daddy. Very boring." I kissed him and his mustache tickled my nose. "Where's Mom?"

"Here's Mom." My mother suddenly appeared behind me.

"Oh! Mom! Dad! Have I got great news—about Winterfest."

"That's old news, honey. Remember? We talked about it last week." Mom's eyes shifted to Dad. He went back to stirring his potatoes.

"You need three hundred dollars to go to Winterfest. That's too much money, Freddie. You know your father and I don't have it. Fixing up this house will take all the extra cash we can scrape together for a long while."

"I know, Mom. I wasn't asking you to give it to me. I understand." I hugged her to show I meant it.

I did understand. The move from Camden had taken most of our savings. But it was something we'd had to do. Dad's arthritis couldn't stand one more snowy winter, so when both my parents were offered jobs in the San Fernando Valley, where the sun almost always shined, we discussed a move, voted on it, and sold our old house. I wasn't sorry, either. I loved California. The only thing I missed in Ohio was Grams. And Dad thought she'd change her mind soon, and move to California, too. She was as lonely for us as we were for her.

"We know you understand, Freddie. You've been great," said Dad. "I just wish there was something we could do."

"Let me think. When do you have to have the money?" Mom had the best head in the family for figuring things out. I think it came from being an algebra teacher.

"December tenth. But it doesn't matter. Because . . ." I wanted to prolong the suspense. "Because . . . I'll have the money. I have a job."

"Since when? Doing what?" Mom asked.

Dad put down his stirring spoon and wiped his hands on his apron. He walked over to me, a grin lighting up his face. He hugged me tight. "Good girl," was all he said.

"Since today. Guess what I'll be doing." I was enjoying being the center of attention.

Mom sat down at the kitchen table to think. She wrinkled up her nose. "Washing cars?"

"Too much competition from the four professional car washes and the dozens of kids who are already in that business. There are more washers than there are cars in this neighborhood. Besides, winter's coming. Who wants a clean car if it's going to get rained on?"

"Okay. Not car washing. . . . Ummm. How about gardening?" Mom looked at me hopefully.

"Me? Garden? Have you forgotten what I did to your ficus tree? Bald—not a leaf—and it only took me a week. Remember your beautiful bromeliad?"

"Oh. My lovely pink-blossomed baby. Those large healthy green leaves. . . ."

"You mean the overfed, overwatered, yellow mess I turned it into while you were visiting Grams in Camden this summer?"

"I guess you're right. It wouldn't be fair to turn you loose on nature. Forget I mentioned gardening." Mom seemed to wilt right before my eyes. Recalling my plant care fiasco made her droop.

"What about baby-sitting?" I asked, changing the subject.

"Baby-sitting? You?" Mom laughed. "You hate baby-sitting. Whenever you stay with little Davey for Aunt Mimmie, you complain about it for days afterward."

"Davey's not so bad. I just like to make Aunt Mimmie think I earned my money."

"You're going to surround yourself with soggy diapers and soiled bibs? I thought you hated talking to people who only came up to your kneecaps." Dad laughed. He was reminding me of what I'd said the last time Aunt Mimmie had asked Mom to ask me to sit.

"Well, I am baby-sitting. And I won't have to say a word to Sammy, if I don't want to."

"Sammy?" asked Dad.

"Sammy Holden. That's who I'll be taking care of, starting tomorrow. He's a chimpanzee."

"He's a what?" Mom croaked.

"She said he's a chimpanzee. . . ." Dad began to laugh. Mom joined him. So did I.

Then I was telling them all about the Holdens, my new job, and Sammy. By the time I'd finished we were all holding our sides, too weak from laughing to eat dinner.

"And it's close enough to our house for me to ride my bike. The best part is, the Holdens are paying me five dollars an hour!"

"Five dollars an hour to baby-sit," Mom repeated. "That's a lot of money—even for a chimpanzee."

"I'll take it!" Dad shouted.

We were off again, laughing hysterically.

I had to rush through dinner. Darren had an important basketball game, and he was taking me to watch him play. I inhaled my lamb chop and some spinach and, after mumbling something to Dad about what a great cook he was when it came to currying an armadillo, asked to be excused. I didn't have much time and I wanted to call Barbara, to see if she and Wiz were going to the game, and to see what she thought of my new job. I had a feeling Darren and the rest of the gang were going to tease me a lot and tell me I was dumb for giving up so many weekends of my senior year for a chimp. I hoped Barbara would be on my side. Thank goodness I had her. Of the girls in our group, she was the only one I could really talk to.

"Wiz and I are going to a wedding rehearsal dinner for his cousin," Barbara said. "Say hi to everyone at the game for us, and tell Darren we wish him luck."

"I will. Barbara?"

"What's the matter, Freddie".

"Nothing's the matter. It's just that . . . I have a job."

"Hey. That's great. What is it?"

"Baby-sitting."

"Can you make enough baby-sitting to pay for Winterfest?" Barbara was the only one I'd told how worried I was about not getting to go because of the cost.

In our group, my family was the least able to afford three hundred dollars. Everyone knew we weren't rich, not that I thought anyone cared. From my first date with Darren, I'd felt accepted by most of his friends. I loved being part of the popular kids. I loved having someone like Darren choose me to be his girl. There was only one small hole in my cloud nine. Woodlake, California was a plush suburb in an affluent area of the San Fernando Valley. Most of the kids I went to school with came from money. Many of them had parents who were doctors, lawyers, even some in show business. I came from Camden, Ohio and my parents were junior high school teachers. They'd had to save and do without for a lot of years to get the kind of house we now lived in, and it needed a lot of fixing up. My new friends were rich, I was not. Until Winterfest, it hadn't mattered.

"Absolutely. Winterfest is a sure thing," I assured her. When I told her how much the Holdens were paying me, Barbara was amazed. And then, when I told her what I was baby-sitting for . . . !

There was a long silence. "A real live chimpanzee? That's fantastic, Freddie. Baby-sitting an ordinary old baby is such a bore."

We laughed together for a few minutes, but then I had to get off the phone. I hung up feeling happy, and hummed all the songs I could think of with monkeys in them, while I dressed for my date with Darren.

Chapter Three

THERE WAS NO DOUBT in my mind how Sandi and Janet felt about the Senior Council's decision to make Winterfest the senior class trip. They were totally ecstatic. In fact, the entire twelfth grade was in outer space. That's all anyone could talk about. Throughout the game, while I watched Darren making baskets and scoring points for our team, and between Sandi's oohs and ahhs over some cute guy on the opposing side, it was Winterfest this, and Winterfest that. Was there life after Winterfest? I wondered.

I tried not to get too involved in their discussion. I still hadn't mentioned my job at the Funny Farm. Not even to Darren when he picked me up for our date. He was so wound up about the game, telling me his game strategy for the night, he didn't notice how quiet I was.

My lack of participation in their conversation didn't seem to be slowing Sandi or Janet down at all.

"I mean, can you believe it? Two whole weeks in Mammouth Mountain, in the snow, with the entire twelfth grade," Janet bubbled. Her long brown ponytail swished back and forth as she tried to follow the ball across the court and talk at the same time.

I envied Janet's thick, shining hair and athletic body. She was in gymnastics and she was good, too. With her slender body and great hair, she looked like the kind of girl my mom called "the high school cheerleader type" from her era—the "nifty fifties."

"You mean, with the *males* of the twelfth grade, don't you," corrected Sandi. "They're the only part of our class that matters."

Sandi was a blonde like me. Well, not exactly like me. She was cute and petite, and what my dad called a platinum bombshell. I, on the other hand, was a dishwater blonde.

"Right." Janet giggled and nodded. Her ponytail flipped up and down.

Sandi pointed to a tall, light-haired boy on the Palms High team. "I wonder if he'd like to transfer to Woodlake? If only for the two weeks of Christmas vacation?"

"Sandi, you're so awful." Janet giggled again. "Mason won't like you looking at other guys."

"Too bad. Mason La Crosse is not my all-to-end-all, and he knows it. I just can't resist big, tall basketball players with curly blond hair." Sandi let her gaze follow the Palms player meaningfully.

Mason was on the basketball team, too, along with Darren and Janet's boyfriend, Richard. But he didn't look anything like the boy Sandi was ogling. Mason wasn't as tall; he was dark and not nearly as handsome. He'd dated Sandi since the beginning of the semester. It wasn't serious, but they were going together—for the time being.

On the other hand, Darren was a tall, curly-headed basketball player. Except for his almost black hair, he fit the image of Sandi's ideal man perfectly. I wondered if she was having trouble resisting my boyfriend, too.

"Aren't you excited about Winterfest, Freddie? You haven't said a word since the game started." Sandi turned so that she was looking right at me. There was no way I could avoid answering her direct question.

"She's too busy watching Darren," Janet answered for me. "You are going, aren't you?"

"Three hundred dollars is a lot to spend for a two-week vacation," I said. "It could take some doing to come up with that much money." I was setting the scene for disclosing my job news, but I changed my mind.

"I wouldn't miss Winterfest for anything. Skiing and sledding and snow, snow, glorious snow." Sandi looked flushed and totally thrilled.

"I think it's the glorious snowmen you're so excited about," I teased.

"I just realized something. What if one of the guys can't go?" moaned Janet, her smile disappearing.

"Anyone in particular?" I asked.

"During the summer, Richard said his mom was going to send him to Paris to spend Christmas with his dad." Janet was madly in love with Richard Armstead. I wasn't too sure how he felt about it, but he seemed to like her, too. She sagged before our eyes.

"Maybe not. Besides, no one is indispensable, Janet. You can always find a substitute." Sandi sounded glib. But then, she didn't love Richard. "Except for Darren, of course. There is no substitute for perfection, is there, Freddie?"

"No. I guess not." To me, Darren was perfect. But it bothered me when Sandi said it.

I was glad when the final buzzer went off and the game was over. Woodlake had beaten Palms, as usual, and was one step closer to the West Valley semifinals. Darren said they'd win the championship again this year. For the last two years, since he'd been on the team, they'd won.

As the Palms guys left the court, the cheerleaders spelled out their team name and gave them a big hurrah, but it was nothing compared to the explosion they gave the Pumas of Woodlake High. I was on my feet with the rest of the spectators yelling myself hoarse.

Down on the floor, I could see Darren accepting claps on the back and exchanging hi-five salutes with his teammates. Just before he went to the showers he turned, scanned the bleachers, found me, and threw me a kiss. Chills went up my spine. He wanted to share his moment of glory with me, Freddie Larson, his girl. Darren Gresham was the handsomest boy I'd ever seen. He was wonderful. Being his girl was the best thing that had ever happened to me. And because I knew his kiss sailed past all the other envious girls cheering madly in the stands, I was melting inside with joy.

After our team left the floor, we made our way down the bleachers and out to the front of the gym to wait for the guys. While we huddled together to keep warm, Sandi and Janet took up their conversation right where they'd left off—more Winterfest.

"I look terrible on skis," said Janet. "I keep falling over."

"I do okay," Sandi said. "I have my own equipment. Darren, Mason, and I were in Blizzard Club last year."

I'd never heard of Blizzard Club, and I guess I gave her a blank look.

"That's a teen ski club. They bus you to local ski runs during the skiing season," she explained. "You should see your boyfriend on skis, Freddie. Darren is the ultimate in handsome snowmen."

"Did someone call me?" Darren walked up to us and slung his arm over my shoulder in the casual way he has. It's as if he's telling the world that I'm his girl. With Darren's arm around me, I felt that I belonged.

"If the snowshoe fits . . ." joked Sandi, flashing him a sparkling smile.

He smiled back. "What are you lovely ladies talking about?"

"Winterfest," I said slowly. Was this the time to tell him about my job? Not in front of Sandi and Janet, I decided.

"Great idea, isn't it? We're going to have the greatest time, Freddie. You and me rolling around in the snow, if you get my drift." He winked, and the four of us laughed at his silly pun.

"Hey, Sandi," Mason called, jogging toward us. Richard was behind him.

"Hey, yourself," Sandi answered. She moved away from Darren to stand beside Mason.

"Hi, Richard," Janet said, giving him a mushy look. Janet was definitely in love.

"Where's the Wiz and Barbara?" Mason asked.

"At Wiz's cousin's wedding rehearsal dinner," I answered.

"Oh, yeah. That bum parties, while we wear ourselves out running our high tops off for the glory of the school. Some buddy," Mason joked.

"So, where shall we go to eat?" asked Richard. "Same place as always? Burgers, Suzy-Qs, and chocolate sodas at Del Rio's?"

"Nah, you guys. Let's do something wild and crazy tonight." Mason scratched his head and pretended to be deep in thought. "Something really daring. Let's go to . . ."

"The same place?" asked Sandi.

"The same place," Darren said.

"The same place?" echoed Janet.

"The same place," Richard said.

"Del Rio's," I shouted, and we all cheered together.

Darren kissed me quickly on the nose, then we ran after the others to his car.

Del Rio's just wasn't any fun that night, but it had to be me; Del Rio's hadn't changed—not in thirty years. I couldn't say exactly what was wrong. The old-fashioned hamburger joint was too crowded and too noisy—just like always. Most of the customers were kids from our school, excited about winning the basketball game, and a little rowdy. But no one ever got out of hand. They didn't want to get tossed out by Del, the two-hundred-and-eighty-pound, ex-professional football-playing, karate black-belt owner. The music blared, colored lights flashed, and everybody talked and ate and had a good time. Everybody, that is, but me.

The six of us squeezed into a booth with more than enough room—for four. The minute we sat down, the congratulations for winning the basketball game started. Guys kept coming over and giving Darren, Mason, and Richard the complicated handshake everyone in Woodlake seemed to know but me. When I tried to do it, I just got confused and messed it up. Girls hung around our table, too, talking with Sandi and pretending not to notice Darren. Sometimes the way they acted around him made me feel good; glad that they thought he was worth wanting, and that he only wanted me. Tonight their flirting made me nervous and uneasy.

I couldn't stop worrying about how he was going to react when I told him about my job. Besides the basketball game, Winterfest was the only other topic of conversation. The big question was, "Are you going on the senior class trip to Mammouth?" Just listening to the other kids talking about it made me edgy. So far Darren hadn't come right out and asked me if I was going. He'd just assumed I was. When the subject finally did come up, I was going to have to tell him how I intended to earn the three hundred dollars I needed to pay my way. Darren wasn't going to like it. Basketball games were usually held on Friday nights.

I was glad when it was finally time to leave.

In the car, I snuggled close to Darren and closed my eyes. I hoped, by pretending to doze, I could avoid any unpleasant subjects for discussion. My plan worked until Darren walked me to my front door.

"What time do you want to go bike riding tomorrow?" Darren slipped his arm around my waist and pulled me to his chest.

I'd forgotten all about going riding. "Well, I . . ."

He lowered his head and pressed his lips against the sensitive skin on my neck. "Is nine too early?" He nibbled on my ear.

My heart pounded, a confused combination of tingles and terror. "I can't, Darren."

"Okay. Tèn. But I refuse to be separated from you any longer than that." He put his other arm around me and pulled me closer.

"Darren, please. You don't understand. I can't go bike riding tomorrow at all. I have to work."

"Work? Why? On what? You mean study? Then we'll come home early. You'll have plenty of time to study before I pick you up for the show."

"Listen to me, Darren, and please don't get mad. I have a job. I have to work all day tomorrow."

"Tomorrow? All day? What about our bike ride?"

"I'm sorry, but I have to. I'll be working every weekend until winter break. I even have to work Friday nights, but I get off early on Saturdays and Sundays. I'm really sorry, Darren, but it is for us."

"What is this? Some kind of a runaround? Are you breaking up with me?"

"No! I love you, Darren. It's just that I have to have a job.
I need the money to pay for Winterfest. Please try to understand. I'd rather spend every day with you, and go to every
single basketball game you play, but I want to go with you to
Mammouth, too. My parents can't afford to send me, so I
have to earn the money myself. I don't even like to baby-sit;
I'm doing it to be with you. I won't have to keep this job
forever. I can quit after Winterfest is paid for."

And by then, I told myself, the Holdens should be finished
filming—I hope. If not, I'd be letting them down by quitting.
Just like Children's Hospital.

"Who are you sitting for?" Darren let go of me and went
to lean against the porch railing. "Your aunt?"

"The Holdens."

"Who are they? How did you find them?"

"Birdie and Noah. They live on a ranch in Canoga Park. I
answered a want ad in the *Daily World*. It pays five dollars an
hour."

Darren turned to face me. The moon shone on his face. He
was still as handsome as ever, but I saw something else in his
face. For the first time, I'd made him really angry. "What
kind of a home do they have? They have to have some pretty
lousy kids. No one makes that much money just to baby-sit
regular children."

"They have a ranch where they raise animals for television
and the movies. I'm going to baby-sit Sammy, their chimpanzee."

"You're kidding, right? A monkey. I don't believe it."

I reached out my hand and touched the sleeve of his
sweater. I wanted him to understand, not laugh at me.

"You're going to spend your weekends and every Friday
night with an ape, instead of me?" He pulled his arm away.

"Don't be mad."

"Why should I be mad? Just because you're never going to

come to another basketball game. Just because you and some chimp are going to make a monkey out of me in front of the entire school.''

"Darren, I'm sorry. It's just that I thought it was more important to go to Winterfest with you. Let's not fight. Please. We can talk about it tomorrow night when we go to the movies. Okay?''

"I don't know.''

"Okay?'' I walked over to the rail and slipped my arms around him, leaning my head on his chest.

"Okay, we'll talk.'' He pulled away and glared down at me. "But you're going to have a hard time making me understand why you would rather spend Friday nights with a chimp than watching me win the West Valley Basketball Championship.'' He started down the steps to his car.

"Darren.''

"What?'' He stopped on the bottom step and turned around.

"You forgot something.''

"Yeah? What?''

"This.'' I put my arms around his neck and pulled his head down until our lips lightly touched. "I love you. Thank you for tonight.''

He moved back up the steps until we both stood on the same one. His arms went around me and his mouth pressed against mine.

When he finally lifted his lips from mine, I sighed. His good-night kiss told me we would work things out.

Chapter Four

"ALL RIGHT, GIRLS AND BOYS, GUYS AND GALS, FRIENDS
AND LOVERS, BUDDIES AND PALS. HERE'S THE NEWS YOU'VE
ALL BEEN WAITING FOR. . . . IT'S SIX A.M. SO, GET UP, GET OUT,
AND GET DOWN. IT'S BOOGIE SATURDAY."

"Oh, shut up," I grumbled, hitting the snooze alarm on
my clock radio. "I don't feel like getting up or getting down.
It may be boogie Saturday to you, but it's Sammy Saturday to
me."

I got up and got dressed anyway.

"What's cookin', good-lookin'?" Dad asked, as I flopped
down on my stool next to him at the breakfast bar.

"Boogie Saturday. I'm bummed out," I mumbled.

"What'd she say?" he asked my mom.

Mom looked up from the French toast she was flipping.
"Your intelligent and articulate daughter has just informed
you that today is her first full day taking care of a chimpanzee
at the Holden Ranch and she is slightly less than thrilled about
it."

''Oh, *that's* what you said. Yesterday you seemed happy about your job, honey. What happened to make you change your mind?''

''It's just that the weekend is supposed to be a person's time off. I've got working woman's depression.'' I couldn't tell my parents that Darren was what had happened. They already felt I was too young to be so serious about a boy.

''Life's a buster, all right.'' Dad smiled sympathetically. Teaching junior high kept him on the fringes of the latest expressions. Mom was much better at using the current slang than Dad was.

''It's bummer, Dad. Life's a bummer.''

''Yeah, that too,'' he agreed. ''Well, if you're going to get out to the Holdens by seven-thirty, and I'm going to get to painting the family room, we'd better eat this stuff.''

''Stuff? My gourmet *pain de France*?'' Mom wailed.

We picked up our forks and dug into the layers of gourmet *pain* Mom heaped on our plates.

''Hi, am I glad you're here,'' Birdie said, opening the front door.

''I'm not late, am I?'' I'd left my house with time to spare.

''Oh, no. You're right on time. I'm the one who's running late. Can you feed Sammy his breakfast, while I shower? Noah is already dressed. He's gone down to the compound to talk with Jon Prince, the boy who works part-time for us feeding the animals and cleaning their habitats.''

Jon Prince? That must have been who was in the old pickup that bathed me in dust yesterday. So, Jon worked for the Holdens, too.

''Maybe you know him? Jon goes to the same school you do.''

''I know who he is. I've seen him around school.'' Jonathan Prince was a senior, too. I didn't have any classes with him, but I knew what he looked like. He was tall, with straight brown hair that stood up a little in front, and not bad-looking. He had a nice smile. He seemed okay, but Jon was a "grinder." That's what all the brains at Woodlake High were called.

"Well, if you get bored hanging around the house today, you can put on Sammy's leash and harness him into his stroller and take a walk down to the compound," Birdie suggested. "I'm sure Jon would like the company. He can show you around."

"That sounds great. Maybe Sammy and I will go out after his nap." If I can get him to take a nap, that is. "Is he in the kitchen?" I could hear his high-pitched monkey chatter.

"In his high chair eating Cheerios. His breakfast is on the counter: some mashed yams, a little chow, and apple wedges. If you think you can handle it, I do have to shower."

"No problem. I can feed Sammy. You go ahead."

Birdie took off down the hall and I went into the kitchen.

"Sammy! You're supposed to be eating those," I scolded. "Not flicking them around the room." In gratitude for my lesson on good table manners, I received a loud raspberry and a damp Cheerio. It stuck to my forehead.

Sammy held up his arms to me, like a child who wants out of his chair.

I shook my head. "Your mother said I should feed you. So that's what I'm going to do." I went to the sink for the bowls that Birdie had laid out.

The biggest bowl had mashed orange stuff in it. "This has to be the yams." Without the marshmallows and brown sugar Mom used to turn them into a Thanksgiving treat, Sammy's yams looked extremely unappetizing, but edible. His apple wedges were cored and neatly arranged on a paper plate; they were turning a little brown but they looked okay. It was the bowl of brown pellets that worried me. I knew the Holdens wouldn't give Sammy anything a chimp shouldn't eat, but the contents of the last dish looked like dog food to me. "Yuck, Sammy. No wonder you want me to lift you out."

Twenty minutes later, with one bowl of orange gook and one of brown smeared on Sammy's face, dripping down his bib onto his high-chair tray, and splattered over the front of my good blue sweat shirt, I'd accomplished what I'd set out to do—feed the monkey.

"Whatever happened to those neat little inventions, the peel-and-eat banana? What a mess." Taking some paper towels from the roll over the sink and wetting a few, I tried to clean up Sammy, who didn't seem to appreciate my efforts one bit.

"How's it going?" asked Noah, poking his head into the kitchen.

I was just taking the stained and soiled Sammy out of his chair. He clung to my neck, blowing bubbles. "No problem," I answered, trying to sound cheerful.

"Don't be discouraged. He always looks like that after a meal. I've always considered feeding Sammy one of the more colorful events in my day."

I looked down at my once powder-blue sweat shirt and laughed. Colorful was a good way to describe feeding Sammy.

"I'm ready," Birdie announced, entering the kitchen. "Did Mommy's baby make all gone?" She tickled Sammy under his chin. "His lunch is in the refrigerator. It's in the red plastic containers marked with his name. He has lunch at noon, then naps for one and a half to two hours. Just treat Sammy like you would any small child, Freddie. Give him water in his training cup. He can have up to two bananas for his snack. Play with him. And change him when he needs it. We did that yesterday, so you know where his diapers and rubber pants are. He can go out, but be sure to keep him on his leash. Oh, yes. His leash and harness are on a hook by the front door. And—"

"And if we don't get going immediately, Birdie, we're going to be late. Tiger's already in the van. You're the last thing I have to load," teased Noah.

"Okay. I know. I'm doing it again. The overprotective mother. I'm ready." Birdie looked so sad as she kissed Sammy good-bye.

"One last thing, Freddie," Noah said, as he was closing the front door. "Regardless of how we act, we realize that Sammy's a chimpanzee, not a child. That means we know that he's both more capable than a child in some things, and less in others. You know how closely you have to watch your little four-year-old cousin?"

I nodded my head.

Sammy nodded his head, too.

"Watch Sammy twice as close. Good-bye, you two. See you about five o'clock." Noah kissed Sammy on the forehead, smiled encouragingly at me, and shut the door.

The lock clicked.

I was on my own.

"Well, Sammy. This is it. What shall we do first?"

Sammy grunted.

I wrinkled my nose. "That's no way to begin a wonderful relationship, kid," I muttered, heading for the nursery to change him.

Without the practiced hands of Birdie to help hold Sammy down, the act of changing his disposable diaper took twice as long and was twice as messy. I wondered how long it would take to get used to that part of my job. My guess was forever.

"Let's go play now, Sammy." I took him by the hand and led him into the family room.

He made straight for the TV and began to suck the on/off knob.

"If you want to watch television, you should ask. You don't have to eat it." I went to the TV to turn it on. The knob was gone. "Sammy! Give me that knob."

Sammy backed away.

"Stay calm. Don't panic. And don't yell at him," I murmured under my breath. And please don't let him swallow that knob, I prayed.

Sammy spit the knob on the floor.

I dove for it. "Thank you," I said with a sigh, and jammed it back on the set, turning it on. Then I put the knob on the mantel until I needed it again.

Sammy crawled up on the couch and snuggled into the pillows to watch the screen.

I sat down beside him.

Watching TV lasted three minutes and then he was off again.

Noah wasn't kidding about having to watch Sammy twice as much as I did my cousin Davey. Actually, ten times as much was closer to the truth.

"What do you want to do now, Sammy?"

He reached up and took my hand, pulling me off the couch. I followed him as he waddled, right foot, left foot, swinging side to side, across the room. In the far corner was a tricycle. Sammy crawled on and grabbed the pedals with his toes. He let go of me to grasp the handlebars.

"Are you going for a ride?" I asked. I suddenly remembered what I'd said to my dad about not having to talk to Sammy if I didn't want to. I seemed to be doing more chatting with him than I'd ever done with Davey.

Sammy turned back his lips in that disgusting monkey smile he liked to make. Then, backing up his three-wheeler, he rode it into the family room's oak-paneled wall.

"Cut that out!" I yelled, as Sammy headed straight for a collision with the telephone table. I grabbed the phone as he hit the table leg and sent the things on top flying.

"Look, you. You were lucky that time. Only some maga-zines and the phone book fell off. But I'm not going to follow you around rescuing the furniture while you play demolition derby. Get off that bike."

"Pffffttt!" A raspberry was obviously Sammy's favorite form of communication.

Sammy abandoned the tricycle and made for the TV again. He put his arms around the set and licked the face of the lady giving the news bulletins. She did look a little bit like Birdie. Maybe those licks were a monkey's way of expressing love. If licks were love, that was one form of the emotion I could do without. I retrieved the on/off knob and made the picture fade to black. If that newscaster only knew; I saved her life, not to mention her face. Sammy wanted to lick her false eyelashes off.

"What now?" I muttered, as I turned to find my mischie-vous charge removing the pages from the Holdens' collection of *National Geographics*. "Sammy, you stop that. I've had enough." I whisked him from the pile of shredded magazine pictures. Bits and pieces fluttered to the floor.

"We are going to have a few rules established. Right now." I carried the squirming, furry little brat to the couch, forcing him to sit in my lap and listen.

Monkey chirps and chimp chatter told me that he was not in the mood for a lecture. Sammy wanted to get down. He wanted to get in as much trouble as possible before his "parents" got home.

It was the old baby-does-in-the-baby-sitter routine.

When the Holdens arrived home from work, while I re-lated the monster antics he'd pulled all day, Sammy would pretend to be a sweet little angel. It was a trick I knew only too well. My cousin Davey invented it to make me look bad in front of my aunt, but she knew better, so his game didn't work.

In the Holdens' case, I didn't know what to expect.

Sammy had never had another sitter. What if the Holdens found their little darling sitting in the middle of total chaos? Their house filled with wreckage and devastation and looking like the aftermath of a tornado? They'd think I wasn't watching Sammy very well. Would they believe that I had tried? Or would they assume I couldn't handle the job? I wasn't going to take any chances with my money for the Winterfest trip. Sammy and I were going to have a little talk—now!

Chapter Five

THINGS RAN MUCH SMOOTHER after our discussion. Sammy wasn't a bad kid (I mean, chimp), just a playful one. I think my tone of voice let him know I was through letting him make a monkey out of me. He shaped up and the rest of the morning was fairly uneventful. Together we constructed a city of shaky wooden skyscrapers. Thanks to Sammy's unsteady stacking our buildings were not architectural wonders. As soon as we got a few of our high-rises constructed, Sammy changed jobs and became a one-man wrecking crew. We put up and knocked down our city until it was time for lunch.

Construction work turned out to be more tiring than I'd thought. After lunch, Sammy went right down for his nap, and I got a chance to look over my civics notes for Monday's test. I settled into Sammy's TV pillows and reviewed the three branches of American government until I felt they were branches from my family tree. I was actually glad when Sammy woke up to keep me company.

"How about a walk, fella?" I asked him, as I changed his

soaking diaper. "We can take our snack down to the animal compound and visit with Jon. Okay?"

It was as if Sammy knew what I was talking about. As if he understood whom we were going to visit. And as if Jon Prince were one of his favorite people, whom he couldn't wait to see. He was superexcited, chirping and jumping around my feet, as I packed up our snack.

I decided to take four bananas with us. Two for Sammy, one for me, and one for Jon. Just in case Jon was hungry and wanted something to eat, too. The bananas looked delicious, big and yellow with no brown spots. If Jon was anything like Darren, he'd want one. Boys always seemed to be hungry. Darren never said no to anything good to eat. I put the bag of bananas into the basket on the back of the stroller.

Clipping on Sammy's leash and hooking him into his halter was a real test of my agility and coordination. When I got his second arm under the strap, he'd pull the first one out. We went around and around. I felt like a Laurel and Hardy comedy. Hardy set up the ladder—Laurel moved it away. Hardy filled up the bathtub—Laurel let out the water. Hardy throttled Laurel—Freddie throttled Sammy. Finally, his leash and halter on and secured to the stroller, we were ready for our walk.

I didn't know what I would find when I reached the compound. A zoo? A lot of animals living peacefully together, two by two, like on Noah's ark? I laughed to myself. Why hadn't I thought of it before? Of course, the Funny Farm was a Noah's ark. What other kind of place would Noah Holden have? I pushed the stroller, listening to Sammy's constant monkey chatter, and speculated about the compound—and Jon Prince.

The tall, leafy trees shaded the path, making me feel like I was on safari in a jungle. All around me, it was deep, dark, and mysterious. A wild animal ranch was a very strange place.

Of course, there was nothing in the world mysterious about Jonathan Prince. He was an A student. He was a "grinder." He had to be boring. It was funny, though, for someone like Jon to be working at the super-unusual Funny Farm. Taking care of wild animals was not exactly an everyday occupation.

I worked at the Funny Farm, didn't I? I wasn't the most unusual person I'd ever met, either.

The packed-dirt path led out past some buildings that could have been feed or storage sheds. Then it wound around between several empty, fenced-in enclosures.

I called out, but no one answered and I didn't see anyone. I went up to several of the empty cages and peered inside. Nothing. One had an old tire hanging from a rope.

"Your playpen?" I asked Sammy. I pushed the stroller again, following the path.

"Where could everyone be?" I wondered out loud. I was beginning to get a creepy feeling. There weren't any animals in the cages we passed.

I was just about to turn back when the growl of an engine made me look around. The beat-up pickup truck from the day before was heading right for us. It pulled to a stop in front of Sammy and me. Jon Prince got out.

"Hi, Sammy," Jon called.

The monkey acted elated. He jumped up and down in his seat, throwing himself from side to side.

Jon walked over to us and knelt down to pat Sammy and talk with him. After Sammy was satisfied with the attention Jon gave him he stopped screeching and shaking the stroller.

I watched Jon chucking Sammy under his chin and cooing to him, and I smiled. They were obviously great friends.

"Hi, Freddie. I'm Jon," he said after a few seconds.

"Hi," I answered.

"Do you know who I am?" he asked. "We go to school together. I've seen you on campus a lot." He looked up at me from his kneeling position.

"I know. I've seen you, too." I suddenly felt very self-conscious.

"Noah said you might be coming down with Sammy to look around."

"Birdie suggested it. She said Sammy likes to come to the compound for walks." I looked at Jon on his knees beside Sammy, smiling up at me.

I smiled back. Up close he didn't seem as boring as I'd expected him to be. Still waters run deep, I reminded myself.

"Oh, he does. Birdie or Noah bring him down to visit me all the time. We're friends. Aren't we, Sam old man?"

The chimp must have recognized his name. Suddenly he was off on another tirade of chatter.

"Okay, okay, calm down," Jon coaxed. "Sorry. I didn't mean to get him so excited. He'll be all right in a few minutes."

"I guess he's glad we came to visit."

"I'm glad you did, too. I was hoping I'd be able to meet you and show you the animals—like the Holdens asked me to, of course." Jon got to his feet quickly. "You want to look around?"

"Yes, thank you. I'd like that," I said.

He led the way along the path without stopping at the empty cages. "These are used for training purposes or for transporting the animals," he explained. "The Holdens try to let the animals live in habitats that resemble their natural surroundings. They're against these kinds of cages."

I nodded my head and pushed Sammy a little faster to keep up.

"This way," Jon said, pointing to a building like the ones

I'd thought were feed sheds. "This is where the Holdens keep their snakes. Noah's really knowledgeable about snakes." We walked past several huge glass cases, each with a dozing snake in it.

I took a deep breath and held it. Snakes! Yuck! Even though I knew better, they looked cold and clammy. But at least the snake house didn't have an animal smell. Maybe snakes looked so slimy because they took so many baths.

I tried to look more interested than terrified, as Jon explained about the inhabitants of each case. I was careful to stay in the middle of the aisle, not too close to the glass cases on either side. Snakes were not my favorite things. I rated my dislike of them right up there with rats, great white sharks, and vampire bats.

"This is Noah's love," Jon said, stopping in front of the largest glass window.

Sammy looked inside and shrieked, covering his eyes. I wanted to do the same.

"What is that?"

"That's Bonnie. She's a South American boa."

"A . . . a boa constrictor?" I remembered by glib pronouncement about baby-sitting a boa for five dollars an hour. I was glad no one had heard me and taken me up on my offer. "It's so huge." I choked. "And ugly."

"She's only about twelve feet long. The Central American variety can be fifteen feet. And you'd better not let Noah hear you call her ugly. She's a beauty queen to him."

"Do you feed her? I'd be afraid to get within ten feet of a snake like that. What if she bit you? I bet you'd die in two seconds."

"The snakes of the Boidae family aren't poisonous. Bonnie doesn't bite her prey to kill it. She wraps herself around it and squeezes it to death. Then she swallows it whole. I feed her mice, but she can swallow a pig without any trouble."

Sammy yelped shrilly. He must have read my mind. If Bonnie could take in a pig with one gulp, a chimp would be no big deal.

"I think we better get Sammy out of here," I said, trying to mask the shivers that were going up my spine. "He doesn't seem too crazy about Bonnie."

"Does she bother you, too?" Jon asked, a knowing smile spreading across his face.

The only thing I liked about Bonnie was that she ate mice, which I didn't like either. I pushed the stroller out into the daylight as fast as I could.

"Nope. I love boas." The warm sunlight felt good after the cool dimness of the snake house.

"I don't believe you."

"It's true," I insisted. "I never lie. I'd love to have one of my very own. A pink one."

"A pink one?"

"A pink *feather* boa, that is."

Jon laughed. "Want to meet Clyde?"

"Yes, I would, very much. He's the famous raincoat lion. I love lions. They have the sweetest faces."

"Then right this way." Jon led us away from the reptile house. "Here. Let me help you," he offered. "We keep this area of the compound covered with gravel to help with rain runoff." He put his hands next to mine on the stroller handle and helped me push.

"Is that him?" I asked, as we stopped in front of a large enclosure of trees and grass, with a manmade stream running through it. I pointed at the huge cat lazing in the afternoon sun.

"I'm afraid so," Jon admitted hesitantly. "That lazy good-for-nothing is Clyde, the king of beasts. Or so I've been told."

The big yellow lion looked up at us, shook his mane,

yawned, and laid his head back down on his paws, closing his eyes.

"He's adorable," I cooed. "A big sleepy pussycat."

"He's just had his lunch and he's sleeping it off. Not that he's a raging man-killer the rest of the time. For Noah and Birdie, he is a big sweet pussycat. They raised him from a kitten. It's a mutual love affair."

"It seems like there's a love affair going on between the Holdens and every animal they own. Especially Sammy."

"You're so right. All the animals are like their children, but Sammy is their baby."

I was beginning to understand Birdie and Noah a little better the more Jon talked about them.

"Set the brake on the stroller and come have a closer look," Jon suggested. "Sammy sometimes gets nervous if he's too close to Clyde. It's better if you park him here, under this tree. We can keep an eye on him from the habitat."

I set the stroller brake and followed Jon up to the enclosure.

"Hello, Clyde," I called to the big cat.

Lions are cute, I thought, wrinkling my nose at the faint smell that filled the air, but they didn't take nearly enough baths—certainly not as many as the snakes did. Clyde's enclosure was spotlessly clean, so he didn't smell that bad—but he didn't smell that good, either.

He didn't even look up.

"You're being rude, Clyde," Jon scolded. "Here a beautiful lady comes to visit and you prefer to sleep."

Jon had called me beautiful. It was only a joke, but it made me feel good.

Clyde yawned again and rolled over on his back. His four huge paws stuck up into the air.

"I must not be a very impressive visitor," I teased.

"Are you kidding? He's overwhelmed. Can't you tell? He rolled onto his back for you—without opening his eyes. That's his most difficult trick."

We both laughed at Jon's joke.

Behind us, Sammy squawked and chattered.

"I think he wants his snack." I started back toward the stroller. "Would you like a banana? I brought extra."

"I'd love one. Thanks."

I looked into the basket. The bananas were gone.

"Hey! Where are they?" I checked the basket again for the missing bag.

"Sammy. . . ." Jon looked at the grinning chimp.

"Sammy!" I looked at him, too.

"Burrupt," said Sammy. His belch was the only answer we needed.

Jon lifted Sammy out of the stroller. The peels from four ex-bananas and one empty bag were squashed under him.

"Thanks anyway," Jon said, holding up the limp peels. "You seem to be all out."

I couldn't stop giggling, but I knew I really shouldn't laugh and encourage Sammy's misbehavior. I shook my finger at him and tried putting on a stern face to correct him. "Sammy Holden, you are a terribly bad little monkey," I scolded.

Sammy licked his fingers and chattered back at me. It was impossible to keep a straight face, even though he didn't look the least remorseful.

"You don't think he'll get sick from eating four bananas, do you?" I asked Jon.

"Not Sam. He's a chimpanzee garbage can. He's always snitching things he shouldn't have from Birdie or Noah. Don't worry about it."

I was relieved.

"By the way, Sammy's a chimp. Chimps are not really

monkeys, they're apes. In Sammy's case, a naughty little ape.''

"I didn't know that—about chimps not being monkeys. I'm glad you told me. But I'd already figured out the part about Sammy being naughty. The bananas are just dessert for the television knob he tried to eat this morning. I can see pint-sized apes can really be a handful.''

"Come on," Jon said. "You do look a little frazzled. I'll drive you back up to the house and you can give me that banana you promised me.''

Together we pushed the cheerful, chattering, and burping Sammy over to the ranch pickup.

As Jon drove us up to the ranch house, I watched him from the corner of my eye. An unsettling guilt washed over me. I'd been hasty and and very unfair to him. I'd made a snap judgment about him, before we'd even gotten to know one another. Well, I was quickly changing my mind. If Jon Prince was a grinder, then grinders were nice people to know.

Chapter Six

"I THOUGHT YOU WANTED to talk about it, Freddie. You were the one screaming for communication. So, let's communicate. Okay?"

"Now, Darren?" I whispered. "In the middle of the movie?"

Sandi and Mason were staring at us, and Sandi gave me the weirdest look. All our friends knew we were fighting.

Darren was so loud the whole theater knew it.

I wanted to die.

Why couldn't I make him understand that I'd taken the job with the Holdens so we could be together at Winterfest? Even if we couldn't spend that much time together now, it was worth the sacrifice. Or at least I'd thought so when I'd conceived my brilliant plan for financial gain. Absolutely nothing was going right anymore—not between Darren and me.

Dad was right; life was a real buster—a heart buster.

"Shhhshhh! Will you please," hissed the woman behind

us. "If you two don't want to see this, then go out to the lobby to fight."

"Before we call an usher," her husband added.

"All right. All right," Darren muttered under his breath. "Some great movie you're missing, mister. Why did we come to see this stinker, anyway, Freddie?"

"Sandi and Mason picked it. Since we were in Mason's van, everyone decided to let them make the choice."

Darren made a noise like a snarl.

He couldn't be mad at me because the movie starred a bunch of chimpanzees. If it had been my choice, I would never have picked *The Planet of the Apes Revisited*.

For the next forty minutes, I ate popcorn, sipped a soda, picked Chewey Fruits out of my teeth, and pretended to pay attention to the screen. When the house lights came up, I was more than ready to leave the theater.

"Neat movie, huh, Freddie?" asked Janet, bouncing up the aisle next to me.

"Neat," I agreed.

She smiled at me, then hurried on ahead to walk beside Sandi, Mason, and Richard. Darren walked away with her.

Barbara, Wiz, and I followed along, three steps behind them, to Mason's van in the back parking lot. Seven of us piled into the back, leaving Mason alone in the front to drive. I sat on the long bench seat in the back of the van next to Barbara and Janet. Darren slouched in the single seat behind the driver's seat. Sandi sat at Darren's feet, leaning back against his chair and sharing the floor with Richard and Wiz. She and Darren were laughing and saying something I couldn't hear. I wasn't jealous but I was beginning to get a little sick of Sandi's too sweet and understanding attitude toward *my* boyfriend. Darren, on the other hand, seemed to be eating it up. The most aggravating thing was their laughter. Darren and I were not only not laughing together; we weren't even talking to one another.

"How does that sound to you?" Barbara was asking me.

"What? How does what sound?" I was concentrating so hard on being upset, I wasn't paying any attention to what was being said around me.

"Going to Goopy's." Janet giggled. "I want a Goopy's Grotesque Three-Flavored Gargantuan."

"That's disgusting, Janet," Sandi told her. "How could you eat something so gross?"

"What are you going to have, Sandi?" asked Wiz.

"The Fantastic Four-Flavored Phantasmagoria with extra whipped cream and double cherries." Sandi's joke dissolved everyone, but me, into peals of hilarious laughter.

"I don't care," I said. "If that's where everyone wants to go, it's okay with me. I don't want anything anyway." I wasn't at all hungry. My stomach was upside down from fighting with Darren; if I ate any of Goopy's horrendous concoctions, I'd probably throw up.

When Mason parked the big silver-and-blue van in the shopping center parking lot and we all got out, Darren was finally able to pull himself away from Sandi long enough to walk with me. Even though he and Sandi seemed to have forgotten it, she was still Mason's girl.

I could hardly believe it when Darren came over to me. He initiated the conversation, and it wasn't about my job, for a change. I was afraid to look at him. Afraid I'd say something wrong again. Afraid I'd make him mad. Afraid I'd break into tears at any moment. I let Darren do most of the talking. When I had to answer him, I kept my real thoughts to myself and acted as if nothing were wrong.

"Are you sure you don't want something? We can share a Gargantuan. Okay?" he asked.

"Okay," I agreed. I didn't want him to think I was mad at him. "I'd like vanil—"

"A Gargantuan. With one scoop of rocky road, one of chocolate chocolate chip, and one of gooey fudge brownie. Heavy on the whipped cream, too," he told the man behind the counter. "That's okay with you, isn't it?"

I nodded. I was an American oddity. I didn't like chocolate ice cream. I'd never ordered it when I was with Darren; I guess he'd never noticed. But since I didn't really want anything anyway, it didn't matter what he ordered. I only had to take a taste or two. I knew Darren would finish the rest.

I watched the man fill the oversized sugar cone, made especially by Goopy's for their Grotesque Gargantuans and Fantastic Phantasmagorias, with three monstrous scoops of chocolate ice cream. The special Goopy's cone was made in a waffle iron and bent around a large wooden cone shaper. Each of the giant-sized cones held over a pint of ice cream.

I'd finished a whole Gargantuan only once in my entire life. That was last August, when I brought Mom and Dad to Goopy's. That day was so hot my dad ate two, one after the other, while Mom and I watched his amazing feat with stunned admiration. Ice cream was my dad's favorite food in the whole world.

"What about tomorrow? Are we all going together to the class car wash?" Mason asked, as we circled the shopping center eating our ice cream. "I don't mind picking everyone up. I'm driving the van there anyway. I'm going to try and get a free wash."

"I can't go," announced Barbara. "I'm working at the hospital."

"Geeze, Barb. I thought you said you'd be off tomorrow," Wiz groaned. He looked at Barbara with sad brown eyes.

"My supervisor asked me to fill in for one of the other girls who's got the flu. I'm sorry, honey. I couldn't say no. The kids would suffer.''

Wiz shrugged and pulled her close. They were like the perfect couple. You could tell how much they cared for each other when you saw how they looked into each other's eyes and acted when they were together.

I remembered Barbara telling me all about her tall and lanky boyfriend on my very first day at Woodlake High School. While we walked around the school and she showed me where my classes were, I got a full report on the wonderful and adorable Ozgood Greenwald. I knew all about him, even before I met him. Barbara even explained to me how he got his unusual nickname, Wiz.

When he was in second grade, a bully had started calling him the Wizard of Ozzie. When he'd finally had enough, Wiz had punched the kid out. That had made him an instant hero with the entire second grade, but the nickname had stuck. Over the years it was shortened to Wiz. Barbara told me he really didn't mind being called Wiz. He actually liked that a lot better than Ozgood or Ozzie.

''I suppose you're working, too,'' Darren said to me. He grabbed my arm and pulled me to a halt. ''The chimp has to be more important than our class car wash.''

The others went ahead as we stopped in front of a travel agency. The window was filled with posters of beautiful places to visit. Places I doubted I'd ever see. I could barely get enough money together to make it to Mammoth Mountain.

''Yes, I have to,'' I whispered. What was the use? No matter how many times I told him why baby-sitting Sammy was so important, Darren refused to listen.

''I figured as much,'' he groused.

''She has to, Darry,'' Sandi said. She'd slowed down and returned to stand in front of the window with us. ''You want her to go to Winterfest, don't you?''

I was beginning to wonder why I'd ever thought Sandi was my friend. She couldn't be anybody's friend. Especially if they had something she wanted. And it had finally dawned on me. She'd never given up on Darren after they'd broken up last year. Sandi Moses wanted him back!

The group turned around and came back to join us.

"Freddie can't come to the car wash either," Sandi announced almost joyfully. "She has to work to earn her fare to Winterfest."

"Oh . . . that's tough," said Richard. "We'll miss you." He sounded sincere.

"Yeah. We'll miss you," Sandi echoed. She didn't sound in the least sincere.

I smiled at Richard.

"You should do what I'm going to do, Freddie," Wiz said. "I know a way to get plenty of money for Mammouth, fast and easy."

"What's that, Wiz?" I asked him.

"I'm selling my wind-surfer."

"Oh, Wiz, you're not," Barbara said.

"Yes I am, Barb. And my roller skates, and my horror comic book collection, and my wetsuit, and my car, and my little brother. If you think I'd let my girl go to the snow alone with a bunch of great-looking ski bums to keep her company, you're crazy. You are going nowhere without me."

Barbara beamed at Wiz's show of mock jealousy. "Will you be serious," she demanded. "You are not selling your brother. I won't let you. Sidney is adorable."

"Sidney? Adorable? Well . . . maybe I'll just sell my wind-surfer. I was going to do that anyway. I'm lousy at wind-surfing. The worst. Besides, I can't swim."

We all laughed.

"I wish I had a wind-surfer to sell . . . or a little brother, for that matter. I'm afraid I have to get the money by honest labor. But thanks for the suggestion." I gave Wiz a quick hug.

"You mean to say your parents can't even scrape up a few hundred dollars to send you? Did you tell them how important this trip is?" Darren leaned over to whisper in my ear.

I shook my head. Darren's dad was a corporation executive. His family had a lot more money for extras than mine, but until now, the difference in our fathers' incomes hadn't even come up. It hadn't mattered at all. How could I make someone like Darren understand how much of a burden spending three hundred dollars on a vacation for me would be for my parents? I had a feeling they would make the sacrifice for me if I asked them. But I couldn't ask.

I looked into the brightly lit windows of the boutiques we passed. My mom couldn't even think about a new dress or new shoes until we finished fixing up our house. The station wagon my family drove was on its last leg. New clothes and a new car for all the Larsons had to wait. We had more important things to do with our money, like replace the furnace before we froze to death, and reshingle the roof before we drowned. Financially, Dad couldn't afford the move we'd made from Ohio to California. But because of his arthritis, he couldn't afford not to make it, either. We'd all had a say in the decision to move. Like my parents, I'd agreed it was the right thing to do. Now I'd have to make do—just like they did.

"I'm sorry about tomorrow, Darren. It's more than just the money. I have an obligation. I took the job baby-sitting for the Holdens, and tomorrow I have to work." There was nothing more to say.

"Sure," he muttered, helping me into the van.

"Hey, Wiz," called Mason from the front of the van. "How about taking a turn at the wheel? It gets awfully lonesome up there without Sandi."

Sandi punched Mason in the arm.

"Sure," Wiz said. He crawled up to the driver's seat, and Barbara followed him to the empty passenger's seat.

Mason sat down on the bench seat with Richard and Janet. He patted the space next to him.

"It's too crowded with four," Sandi complained, starting to take the single seat Darren had used before.

"Then sit in my lap," Mason told her, pulling her onto his knees.

Sandi sat in his lap, but she looked as if she were in pain. Her eyes kept darting to Darren.

I looked at Darren, too. If he cared where Sandi was sitting, it didn't show on his face. He seemed preoccupied. He looked a million miles away. Instead of taking the empty single seat, he flopped down next to me on the floor. Absentmindedly, he put his arm around me and leaned back against the van wall.

I wondered what he was thinking about. I hoped he was coming to some decision about my job. I hoped with all my heart he was deciding that it was for the best. And that I really was doing it for us.

As if he'd heard my thoughts, he pulled me closer to his side and kissed me lightly on the cheek.

My heart soared. Darren finally understood. He had to see that I was only doing what I had to do. He wasn't mad at me any longer. At last we weren't going to argue anymore.

I raised my face to his and closed my eyes. His hand slipped behind my neck and pulled my head toward his. I felt him relax as our lips met. Our kiss was warm and exciting, made my head spin—like always. Nothing had changed between us.

"Forget the car wash, Freddie." Darren kissed me again, his lips moving against mine. "I'm sorry we had a fight."

"Me too," I murmured.

"You feel good," he whispered, pressing his mouth to mine once more.

"Ummm," I agreed, returning his kiss.

I opened my eyes slowly and looked around the van.

Barbara and Wiz were laughing and talking up front.

Janet was curled up against Richard. They were whispering and sharing little kisses.

Mason had his arms around Sandi, but she wasn't paying much attention to him. She was watching Darren and me instead.

Darren looked up to see what had taken my mind off of kissing him. He looked directly at Sandi.

With a smile, Sandi turned toward Mason, put her arms around his neck, and kissed him passionately.

If she did it to impress Darren, he didn't seem to notice; he began to nibble on my ear.

"Why don't I come over to the ranch after the car wash to see you?" he whispered in my ear. "You can show me around."

"I don't know, Darren. I should ask the Holdens first."

"Ask them if it's okay when you get there. If they say no, I'll just go home. Okay?"

His lips brushed my cheek and nuzzled my neck. I couldn't think. "Okay," I answered. "Ummm . . . yes. Okay."

"I should meet my competition, shouldn't I?"

"Your competition?" Jon Prince's image suddenly flashed into my head.

"Sammy . . . the chimp." Darren kissed my neck again.

"Oh, Sammy. Of course, Sammy."

"Who else is there?" Darren asked.

"No one, and you know it," I answered quickly. "No one at all."

The image of Jon's face smiled at me. It took a concentrated effort to get it to fade from my mind.

Chapter Seven

SAMMY AND I HEARD the chug of the ranch truck as it rumbled up the dirt road to the house. By the time it pulled up at the front porch and stopped, Sammy was like a jumping bean bouncing around on his changing table. It was a struggle to keep him from turning the table over. Chimps are stronger than they look and he fought me all the way. The last thing my little charge wanted was to waste time letting me dress him. He knew Jon was in the truck. He didn't want clothes. He wanted Jon.

Quickly, with Sammy berating me in chimp chatter, I slipped his rubber pants over his wiggly bottom and tucked in the ends of his disposable diaper. I tucked and he untucked. He kept pulling my hands away and trying to climb up into my arms.

"Cut that out, Sammy," I warned, putting on a good show of determination. "If you don't let me dress you, you can't visit with Jon."

Mentioning Jon's name was a mistake. It only excited him more. I wrestled Sammy back on to the changing table.

"Gotcha!" I shouted when I had him pinned and finally got his arms into his T-shirt. "There." I stood Sammy up to admire my work. "You look nice. All ready for company." I let out a sigh of relief. Dressing Sammy at any time was a chore, but when he was anxious to see Jon, it was a nearly impossible task.

Sammy wriggled excitedly in my arms as I carried him to the front of the house. His enthusiasm was contagious. I didn't know why I should be, but I was sort of excited about seeing Jon, too. I walked a little faster when I heard him slam the door of the pickup. My hand was already on the knob when his heavy work boots clattered across the worn porch boards. I turned it before he rang the bell.

Sammy clapped as I opened the door.

"Hi. I just thought I'd come by and see how you and the furry gnome, here, were getting along." Jon smiled at me. "Oh. And I brought something for Sammy." He held out a red, white, and blue rubber ball. "Official Olympic water-polo ball," he explained. "You better start practicing now, Sam. You wouldn't want to be the team's weak link, would you?"

Sammy took the ball, then planted one of his wet excuses for a kiss on Jon's cheek.

"Don't mention it," Jon said, kissing him back.

Sammy licked his new ball and then threw it at Jon.

"Come on over here, you little devil." Jon held out his arms and Sammy went right into them. "How you doing, little fella, huh?" he whispered in Sammy's ear.

Sammy responded with a blood-curdling squeal of joy.

"That's good," Jon said, laughing. He pulled his ear away to protect his hearing.

"We're fine. He hasn't worn me down—yet," I said. "But he's closing in on me fast."

Jon laughed again. "Don't give up, Freddie. You can handle this half-pint. I know it."

"Well, thanks for the vote of confidence. I hope you know what you're talking about." I watched Sammy licking and kissing his new ball. Sammy was certainly not your average baby-sitting charge.

"I didn't expect to see you here today," said Jon. "I kind of thought you'd be going with your boyfriend to the class car wash."

"How could I? The Holdens had a call today. I had to be here with Sammy. How come you didn't go?"

"Don't know. I guess I don't have a lot of interest in the social side of school." He took Sammy to the couch in the family room and sat down. Sammy was still in love with his new toy, and too preoccupied to want to make mischief.

"What do you have an interest in? Besides studying, that is? I know you're in the Honor Society." I sat down on the couch with them.

Sammy wedged in between us.

"The ocean. I snorkle. I'm a certified scuba diver. Most of the things I do for fun, I do underwater. I'm going into marine biology after college. I guess I'm part fish. Being in Honors is no big deal. I like school, and I like to study. My dad used to tell me before he died, 'A day in which you haven't learned at least one new thing is a day wasted.' "

"I'll bet you don't waste too many days."

"No. Not too many. I've become kind of a fanatic about accumulating knowledge. I even read the encyclopedia for pleasure."

"I do, too, sometimes," I admitted. It was the truth. It came from having two schoolteacher parents. Ask one of them a question and you found yourself reading the encyclopedia. It was habit-forming. "But you have to admit, the characters may be fascinating, but the plots are thin.''

Jon laughed. ''You sure are funny for a chimpanzee baby-sitter.''

''For your information, in my line of work a sense of humor is mandatory, or . . .''

''Or you'd go ape, right?'' We were laughing again.

''Seriously, Jon, I should think you'd want to go to our first fund-raising project. I really wanted to be there.'' For more reasons than one, I admitted only to myself. ''Don't you feel any obligation to help earn some of the class's cost for Winterfest?''

''Not really. I'm not going.''

''You're not!''

''Nope. It'll cost too much. I'm saving my money for college. Three hundred dollars will buy a lot of marine biology books. Even with a scholarship, my going to the university is going to be a hardship on my mom.''

''But Winterfest will be our most important senior activity—except for the senior prom. That's why I'm work-ing: for the money to go with our class to the snow.'' I couldn't believe he meant what he said. He didn't want to go with everyone else to Mammouth!

''I doubt I'll go to the prom, either. That can cost a bundle, too. Besides, there's no one I'd want to spend that much money on. Unless . . .''

Was Jon going to ask me to go to the prom with him? But he knew I had a boyfriend. Or did I? I'd know the answer to that if Darren showed up after the car wash. I knew there was no point, but I couldn't stop worrying and wondering if he would come. What I needed now was something else to worry about. Like what I was going to say to Jon, if he really was planning to ask me to the prom. I didn't want to hurt his feelings.

"Unless . . . you would like to be my date, Sammy," Jon concluded.

The chimp heard his name and began to screech again.

"I think that means you have a date," I said happily.

"I guess," Jon said, his blue eyes twinkling. "Maybe you and Darren Gresham will double with us. I don't have a car. Even though Noah and Birdie let me use the ranch pickup whenever I want to, I'd hate to embarrass Sammy by taking him to the prom in such an old rattletrap."

"Why not? Darren would love to double. I'm sure of it." Why had I said that—even as a joke? I didn't know how Darren felt about anything anymore; he was acting so strange. The way things were now, I couldn't be sure we'd even be going to the prom together. "Actually, I don't know how Darren will feel about Sammy."

But before she'd left that morning, Birdie had given me permission for Darren to come and meet Sammy. Maybe I'd get lucky. Maybe Darren and Sammy would love each other.

"I'll let you know. Okay?"

"No hurry. I still have to rent a tux; and Sammy needs to find a dress. Or . . . am I going as the girl?"

Jon's quick humor and warm smile helped me forget how upset I was over my floundering love life. I worried that Darren wouldn't come to see me today after all. I worried that he would. Mostly I worried that he'd hate Sammy and be even madder that I was giving up so much of our time together to baby-sit him.

"As much as I'd like to stay and talk, I do have work to do. Clyde and Taurus are first on my list of jobs that I should shovel off to."

"Shovel, huh?" That made me laugh.

"I'll come back this afternoon, okay, Sam?" Jon stood up with Sammy clinging to a back jeans pocket.

"Come after Sammy's had his nap—about three. He'll be ready to play by then."

If Darren came over, he'd said it wouldn't be until one o'clock—after he and the gang had lunch. I couldn't have planned it better. Darren and Sammy could meet, say hello, and say good-bye. Then, at one-thirty, Sammy would take his nap.

"Great. I'll make three my lunch hour," Jon agreed.

"Me too. I usually eat while Sammy naps; I'll make us lunch and wait so we can eat together."

I didn't say anything about Darren coming to meet Sammy and visit with me, which meant I wouldn't be taking a lunch hour. It didn't seem important for Jon to know. Darren should be gone by three, anyway.

Darren was late. By one-thirty I was almost sure he wasn't coming at all. I had Sammy all ready to go down for his nap, but I hesitated to put him to bed. Once he was asleep I couldn't wake him to meet Darren; Sammy was always irritable and difficult to handle when he first woke up. I wanted Darren to see my charge at his best.

At two, I knew I couldn't put off Sammy's nap a moment longer. He was rubbing his eyes and yawning. Birdie had warned me not to let him sleep past four o'clock, ever. Then he would be up most of the night. I picked Sammy up and started for his nursery.

I was in the process of pulling up the blanket when the unmistakable roar of Darren's Fiat vibrated through the house. My heart began to thump.

"It's him," I told Sammy, pulling him out of the crib and running to the front door.

I didn't wait for Darren to knock. By the time he'd stopped his car and turned off the motor, I was out the front door and waiting on the porch for him. Sammy wiggled away in my arms.

"That's it, huh?" Darren stopped at the bottom step. "It looks dangerous."

"Oh, Darren. Don't be silly. Sammy's not an 'it.' He's a 'he.' And he won't bite." That wasn't exactly the truth. "Well . . . he does bite sometimes. But not much. And not if he likes you. It's just that he's sleepy; he waited for you and now he's late for his nap."

"Then stick him in bed." Darren inched up the steps slowly.

"I will, after you two meet properly."

"Hi, chimp. I'm Darren. Nice to meet you. Have a good nap."

"Darren, quit teasing and come in." I led the way to the family room couch.

Darren followed a few steps behind us. He waited until I put Sammy on the couch, then pulled me quickly into his arms. His clothes were still damp from washing cars.

"Now, that's much better," he said, nuzzling my neck.

Sammy screeched jealously, while Darren kissed me hello.

You see, Freddie Larson, I told myself. You do have a boyfriend. You were worried for nothing. Wet shirt and all, I snuggled into Darren's arms.

"Was the car wash a success?" I asked him.

"Fantastic. We must have washed a million cars. A million and one. Old Rumplemeyer made us do his crummy wreck of a Mercedes twice. Said we missed the tires and under the fenders."

"He didn't!" I laughed.

"You better believe it. Who else do you know would expect you to wash *under* his fenders?"

"Only Rumplemeyer," I agreed.

"You got it. Sandi and I must have spent at least an hour on Rump's car alone. But we had fun anyway. You missed a great time."

I'll bet I did. But not my dear friend Sandi. It appeared she'd had a super time. She wanted Darren, I was sure of it. And she was jealous of me, because I had him. All along, she'd been planning to move in. And now that I'd taken a job and conveniently stepped out of the picture, now that I couldn't be around every minute to protect my interests, I'd made it easy for her. She obviously felt that it was now okay to go after my boyfriend. Well, I wasn't going to let her get away with it.

"What do you do here all day? You their cleaning lady, too?"

"Darren! I don't know if the Holdens have a cleaning lady or not. I only have to clean up after myself and Sammy, when I'm with him."

"Come here, little monkey," Darren coaxed. "Darren wants to give you a big hug."

Obviously, Sammy didn't like Darren one bit. He turned back his lips and shrieked. Then Sammy sprang at Darren.

"Get him off! Get this little ape off of me, Freddie! For Pete's sake, he's eating my shirt."

Sammy had jammed the collar of Darren's expensive knit shirt into his mouth. He slurped away happily.

"No he's not. He's only sucking it." I reached out to lift Sammy off.

"Great. I don't want it sucked." Darren literally tore Sammy away from his shirt. Part of his collar came away with the chimp.

"Look what he did!" Darren yelled. "Get this Dennis the Menace off of me, right now."

"I can't, if you won't stand still." I followed Darren as he backed away from me.

As he moved back, he had his hands on Sammy's waist and was trying to disengage him by pushing in the opposite direction.

"Darren, no! Don't! Stop!"

Sammy hung on like a wood-shop vise.

Darren pushed harder. He only succeeded in getting his collar torn off—just before he fell over the coffee table behind him.

Darren yelped.

Sammy yelped louder. He was terrified. He let go of Darren. And with the collar of Darren's shirt dangling from his mouth, he skittered across the family room and into the kitchen.

Darren was on his feet and going after Sammy.

"No!" I shouted. "Let me get him. You're only scaring him."

"I'm going to kill that ape. Look what he did to my new shirt."

"Darren . . . wait!" My warning came too late.

From where I stood, I could see Sammy picking up the plastic bowl of fruit salad I'd made for Jon's and my lunch. Darren didn't realize what was happening until the little chimp delivered the contents of the bowl to him—in the face.

Sammy took advantage of the confusion to escape. While Darren picked fruit salad off his face and out of his hair, the chimp dropped the bowl and made a run for it.

I followed him as he made for the front door.

Had I locked and chained the door? I couldn't remember. Birdie had warned me. . . .

When I reached it, the front door was open and Sammy was on the porch.

"Just let me get my hands on him," Darren hissed. He stepped out onto the porch a second behind me.

"No, Darren. Don't lunge at him. You're scaring him. He doesn't understand."

"He'll understand this. . . ." Darren raised his hand and tried to whack Sammy.

Sammy opened his mouth. He was going to bite Darren.

I was too frightened to move. What would Darren do if Sammy bit him? I didn't know what to do.

"Don't you dare!" Jon shouted.

That's when I saw the pickup parked beside the little red Fiat.

Jon ran up onto the porch and grabbed Sammy off the porch rail before Darren could hit him.

"You touch this chimp and I'll flatten you, Gresham."

"Talk's cheap, grinder." Darren took a step closer.

"Take Sammy, Freddie." Jon pulled the chimp's clinging fingers from around his neck and thrust him into my arms.

I hugged the whimpering, frightened creature to me, Darren's collar still clutched in his mouth.

Darren looked daggers at Sammy, who hid his face under my arm. Then Darren glared at me.

Everything was going wrong. I was so hurt and angry, I wanted to cry.

"Yeah, Freddie. You take the ape. And he"—Darren pointed at Jon—"can take you."

Darren stomped off the porch and got into his car. It took several tries before he was able to get it started. Then he tore off down the dirt road with a roar. Black clouds of exhaust mixed with the swirling dust, and rocks and pebbles scattered in his wake.

Birdie and Noah aren't going to like this, I thought, as I watched the red sports car speed away. Darren would never be allowed out to the ranch again. Not that I thought he'd care much.

"Everything that could go wrong did," I said, remembering all the terrible things that had happened. Big fat tears began to stream down my cheeks.

Jon rushed to my side. He pulled me and the quivering Sammy into his arms.

"It wasn't your fault, Freddie. Don't cry. I'll tell Birdie and Noah how Darren was threatening Sammy. They won't be mad at you. There was no way you could have known how Darren would act."

Sammy clung to me, and Jon smoothed back my hair from my face.

"Jon . .." I gasped for breath through subsiding tears. "Jon . . . you don't understand."

"Yes I do. But you shouldn't cry over a creep like Darren Gresham. He isn't worth it."

The memories of Darren with fruit salad dripping down his face and of Sammy chewing up Darren's collar sprang into my head.

"I'm not crying, Jon. Honestly, I'm not." My tears of laughter began again.

Chapter Eight

IT WASN'T EASY to be the same sweet and friendly good old Freddie with Sandi. I'd have done anything to avoid sitting with her and Janet at lunch. But Barbara was still my best friend and still part of Sandi's group; so when Janet waved to us, Barbara headed in that direction. I had no choice but to go along.

I dragged my feet slowly, trying to control my impulse to make a run for it. There was no way I could pretend to be civil to Sandi, now that I was on to her. A lump the size of a Ping-Pong ball was growing inside my throat.

Stay calm, I told myself. Darren is your boyfriend, not hers. She's the outsider, not you. She's the one who needs to play games, not you.

Trying to stay cool, while my stomach did Olympic gold medal-winning triple-flip high dives. I sat down and unpacked my lunch.

What rotten planning. I stared incredulously at my food. Not today, when I already felt as if I were choking on table-tennis balls. Not . . . peanut butter and bananas on rice crackers! Glue and Styrofoam, Mom called my favorite lunch. And I had forgotten to buy milk before sitting down. I was a goner. I took a bite and swallowed hard. The Ping-Pong lump was still there, but now it was bigger.

"What's that loser waving at?" Sandi hissed under her breath. Her eyes darted right and left to indicate she meant someone sitting on the benches across from us.

I turned to see what loser she was referring to. It was Jonathan Prince. He saw me look up and waved again. I waved back.

"You buddy-buddy with the grinders now?" Sandi asked in a snide tone of voice.

"Jon's nice," I squeezed out around the rice cracker wedged in my throat and the peanut butter stuck to my teeth.

Barbara gave me a strange look, as if she were trying to tell me something. No one else noticed as she slowly shook her head. She already knew about my working with Jon. She also knew the whole story about Darren coming to see me after the car wash. Her meaningful look was to let me know that no one else had heard about the latest disaster between Darren and me, and to warn me not to say anything.

Darren must not have told anyone. Obviously, he wasn't too eager to relate his meeting with Sammy—or Jon—to our group.

I knew I'd never say anything about it—especially to Sandi.

"Is he in one of your classes?" Janet asked. "He's kind of cute." She glanced over at Sandi and quickly smiled apologetically. "For a grinder, I mean."

"He's a wimp," Sandi informed her. "I don't even have to know him to know that. All grinders are wimps." Sandi stared right at me as she spoke. She dared me to deny it or defend Jon. We were in some kind of a contest. She against me. I was sure Darren was the first prize—winner take all.

"Jon Prince is extremely nice," I repeated. "He works at
the ranch for the Holdens, too. We're friends." I stared back
at Sandi defiantly. Jon was nice, and I wasn't going to let her
say anything mean about him.

"Does he baby-sit a chimpanzee, too?" asked Janet.

"No. He takes care of the other animals in the trained-
animal compound."

"Isn't he like a zookeeper?" Barbara asked.

"Something like that," I agreed.

"Isn't that dangerous?" She sounded concerned.

"I don't think so. The animals have all been trained by
Birdie and Noah and seem very used to humans. Jon's
worked for the Holdens for a long time and seems to know
what he's doing. If his job were dangerous, I don't think the
Holdens would let him work with their animals and risk his
life. They like Jon too much. And Birdie told me they needed
special permits and expensive insurance to run the ranch. I
don't think they'd take any chances."

"Know what I think, Freddie? I think if I were going with
someone as super as Darren, I wouldn't spend too much time
with that grinder. He may be nice, but he's not worth losing
Darren for. Right, Janet?" Sandi looked smug.

"Oh, no. Me either. Sandi's right."

I was beginning to wonder if Janet ever had a thought of
her own, one that Sandi hadn't given her. I doubted it.

"Freddie, what's Jon doing now?" asked Barbara.

I looked across the quad and laughed.

Jon sat on the bench, his legs folded Indian-style under
him, peeling huge imaginary bananas. He peeled one, threw
the nonexistent peel over his shoulder, and stuffed the invisible banana into his mouth. Then he peeled another. Then he
peeled a third banana. His cheeks were puffed out, ready to

burst. Before he pretended to peel the fourth banana, he held it out to me. Then he changed his mind about sharing and shook his head. He peeled his last banana greedily and jammed it into his overfilled mouth. After one gigantic swallow, he scratched himself under his armpits, picked up the remains of his sack lunch, and left.

"What a jerk," Sandi said. "What was all that about?"

"Real dumb, huh, Sandi?" said Janet.

"What was he doing?" Barbara asked again.

"Oh, nothing. He was imitating Sammy. Sort of a joke between us," I answered.

"You and the chimp?" asked Janet.

"Or you and the grinder?" Sandi asked maliciously.

I didn't bother giving her an answer.

She must not have expected one. She turned her back on me and began a whispered conversation with Janet. Whatever they were saying must have been extremely funny. They put their heads together and became hysterical with laughter.

Barbara and I went on talking about my job and Sammy and Jon. She was the only one who thought what I was doing sounded like fun. "It's so exotic," she said. "I'll bet no one else in the whole world has ever baby-sat a chimpanzee. It must be a wonderful experience."

"It's an experience all right. Remember how we used to complain about the antics some of the ambulatory patients at Children's Hospital got up to? Compared to Sammy, they were little angels."

"You do like your job, though, don't you?"

"I suppose I'm starting to. I guess I am getting a little bit attached to that big ape."

"Jon?" Barbara asked slyly, her eyes wide.

"Barbara! Stop that," I whispered. "Darren and I are still going together. You know I meant Sammy."

"Are you really?"

"Am I really what?"

"Still going with Darren."

As if he'd heard his name called, Darren appeared and sauntered up to the bench. "Mind?" he asked and wedged himself between Sandi and me.

I minded plenty. I minded his starting a conversation with Sandi and acting as if I weren't even there. I could feel tears of hurt and humiliation welling up in my eyes. I was so stunned I sat there like the last living polar bear all alone on an Arctic iceberg with nothing to do but wait for the spring thaw. If it hadn't been for Barbara's efforts to have an in-depth discussion with me, I'd have died of loneliness on my floating ice cube. She saw my face and saved my life.

"Come on, Freddie. You almost forgot your meeting with Mrs. Hasselhorner." She grabbed me by the arm and pried me off the bench.

"Mrs. Hasselhorner?" What was she talking about?

"You haven't forgotten about her asking you to come in and discuss that special science report you're planning on doing for your term paper, have you?"

"My report . . . ?" Suddenly the wires in my brain made a connection and a light flashed on. "No. Of course not. What time is it? I should have watched the time. Thanks for reminding me. See you all later." I was off the bench in a hasty escape.

Barbara was right behind me.

"A report on chimps?" Darren asked as I hurried away.

"Or on grinders?" called Sandi, her laughter echoing loudly.

I raced for the crowded safety of the main building.

"Do you still think you and Darren are going together?" Barbara asked when I finally ran out of steam and leaned against a bank of lockers to catch my breath.

I shook my head in despair. Tears began to stream down my face. "I don't know what to think, Barb. I only took my job at the Funny Farm so I could be with Darren in Mammouth. Now he hates Sammy and my having to baby-sit for him. Why? Why didn't I pick some other line of work? I just knew baby-sitting would be a mistake. I knew it was no job for me. I hate baby-sitting. I do. Now more than ever. Oh, Barbara. Everything is so messed up."

"Maybe you took the right job, but for the wrong reason. Look, Freddie. It's none of my business, but Darren's . . . Oh, never mind. Forget it. Everything'll work out for the best in the long run. I'm sure of it."

"You are?" I asked hopefully.

Barbara leaned over and wiped my eyes with the rumpled tissue she pulled from her jacket pocket. "Here," she said, handing it to me. "You look awful. Blow your nose and go to class. Do you want me to meet you somewhere after school?"

"No. I'm okay," I sniffled, wiping my eyes.

"Are you sure?"

"I'm sure. Besides, nothing's changed between Darren and me. Really. I always meet him outside the gym gate to drive home. I'm going to wait there for him just like I always do. I know he'll come get me after school on his way to the parking lot."

"Freddie, maybe today . . ."

"I've got to wait for him, Barbara. I've got to talk to him."

Barbara shrugged and nodded. "Okay, see you, then. I've got to run."

As she hurried away, I thought I heard her mumble something about "making a big mistake."

I turned toward the stairs to go to my next class and bumped into Jon Prince.

"Excuse me," we apologized at the same time.

"I didn't see you." My explanation was drowned out as the bell for the end of lunch rang.

Immediately, the halls swarmed with students madly rushing in every direction. Jon and I, standing a few feet away from the staircase, were in the line of the oncoming traffic. People jostled for position, pushing and shoving us to get to the stairway.

"My fault," Jon said. "I'm afraid I was watching where I was going."

"You mean you weren't watching, don't you?" I corrected.

"Oh, no. I *was* watching. I deliberately bumped into you to get you to stop."

"You did? Why?"

A familiar giggle behind me made my head turn.

Sandi . . . and she was walking arm in arm with Darren.

"I want to ask you something." Jon's hand brushed mine.

"What?" My attention was still on Sandi with her arm draped through Darren's.

They were headed our way. Darren was talking while Sandi hung on his every word.

I forced myself to look away.

"Would you mind if I called you sometime? At your house?"

"Called me?" I felt a pointed elbow in the small of my back. I fell forward into Jon's arms.

"Oh, Freddie. I am sorry," Sandi simpered as she dragged Darren past me and up the stairs.

Darren didn't even look at me, but he'd seen me. I knew he had.

"Call you tonight, maybe?" Jon continued, unaware of the nasty encounter I'd just faced.

"Sure. Why not? I'd like you to call me, Jon."

"Great. I'll talk to you, then." He squeezed my hand, then stepped into the crowded hall traffic and disappeared.

Suddenly I was swamped with guilt. Why had I told Jon it was okay to call? Because I was so upset over Darren and Sandi? No matter what, I still loved Darren; and it really wasn't okay. I was being unfair to Jon. Using him to get even with Darren. How could I do that? When Jon called, I'd remind him that I was going with someone and I wasn't really free to date him. We could be friends, I'd tell him, but nothing more. I'd say I was sorry if I'd let him think otherwise.

I felt better. I pushed back my shoulders and joined the crowd threading its way up the stairs.

For the rest of the day I kept promising myself everything would be all right. I would meet Darren after school. We would talk. I would reassure him. Show him how much I loved him. We would work out our problems. He was just jealous of my job and using Sandi to make me jealous, too, but I had no intention of doing the very same thing with Jon Prince. He was too nice a guy to be treated like that. If I had to, I would quit my job to keep Darren. I'd find another way to get the money for Winterfest.

When the final bell rang I didn't even stop at my locker to drop off the books I didn't need. Instead, I ran for the gym gate.

I leaned against the chain-link fence and waited for Darren for almost an hour, but he never came out of the gym. When I walked over to the student parking lot, his car was gone. I tried not to think about it, but I knew he'd left school a different way to avoid seeing me. Tears filled my eyes as I stumbled from the parking lot to the sidewalk. I pulled out Barbara's soggy, nearly destroyed tissue and wiped away my tears.

"She tried to tell me that I was making a big mistake—I should have listened." I wiped my runny nose.

Should haves—should haves—should haves, I berated myself with every step of the three-mile walk to my house. Each step brought a brand-new tear.

"What am I going to do? What am I going to do?"

I went through the motions of setting the table for dinner, but I needn't have bothered. At five o'clock Mom called to say she and Dad were stuck at a faculty meeting and wouldn't be home to eat. She said to fix whatever I wanted, they'd grab something on the way home. I didn't want anything, but I made scrambled eggs and a piece of toast. I nibbled at my tasteless meal and pushed the eggs around on my plate until they were too cold to eat. Finally, I quit wasting time and threw the remains into the garbage. Then I did my few dishes and went to my room to finish my homework. I was up to my eyeballs in the United States Supreme Court system when the phone rang.

"It's Darren!" I shouted. I leaped up from my desk, books and papers cascading to the floor, and ran to answer the ringing instrument.

"Hello. Is Freddie Larson there, please?"

"This is Freddie." My heart sank.

"Hi. It's me, Jon."

"Hi, Jon. It's nice of you to call." It's funny the things you automatically say over the phone just to be polite.

"You said it would be all right. It is, isn't it?"

"Sure. I'm glad you did." I hadn't said that just to be polite—I was glad.

"You doing homework?"

"Yes . . . civics. I hate it. It's so boring. I liked eleventh-grade history a lot better."

"Me too. Look, Freddie. I won't keep you. I've got a ton of homework, too. I was just wondering if you'd like to go somewhere with me this coming Thursday?"

"What about school?"

"Don't you remember? The teachers have to get their records up-to-date for quarter grading, so we don't have school."

"Right. I'd forgotten."

"Well . . . would you?"

"I would. Yes. I'd like to go somewhere with you on Thursday. Anyplace you'd like." I wasn't just being polite—I was being downright friendly. But right now I needed a friend. Besides, he hadn't said "date." He'd only said "go somewhere." Friends go places together all the time, don't they?

"You would? Hey, that's great. I'll pick you up at ten in the morning. Wear jeans or something old. That's great, Freddie, and thanks."

"Thank you, Jon—for asking me. I'll see you tomorrow at school."

"Okay. I'll see you, Freddie. Have a nice night. Good-bye."

"Good-bye, Jon. You too." I smiled warmly into the phone, although I knew he couldn't see me. It didn't matter. For the first time all day I felt like smiling.

As I hung up the phone my smile faded a little. What had happened to the promise I'd made myself not to use Jon? Where had my resolve gone? I could call my going out with Jonathan Prince anything I wanted to. But I'd just accepted a date with him while I was going steady with Darren.

Barbara's "Are you?" flashed across my brain.

Was I? I didn't know anymore. I did know I wanted to go with Jon. And I knew it felt good to smile again.

Chapter Nine

"THANK HEAVEN IT'S THURSDAY," I told Suris, my cuddly purple rhino. I tossed him onto my newly made bed to lie among his fellow stuffed animals. "I couldn't have lasted much longer." I'd been a mental case all week—happy, unhappy, on the verge of tears or laughing at nothing.

I acted so weird at school, Barbara suggested that instead of working at the Funny Farm, I should consider having myself committed to one. There were several teachers, from whose classes I'd exited in tears for no apparent reason, who would have agreed with my friend.

One minute I'd be really depressed because Darren didn't call and whenever I saw him at school, which was rarely, he was with Sandi. Then the next minute I'd be up again, feeling happy because I was spending Thursday with Jon.

Too happy, Barbara decided, graciously pointing out that overcompensation was one of the more obvious signs of a severe mental disorder in teenagers.

My manic-depressive moods were beginning to drive my parents crazy, too. Mom got so fed up with me Tuesday night, she offered to help me pack if I wanted to run away. I didn't blame her. I asked her to tuck me into bed, instead. I felt better after she kissed me good night.

So, ignoring my good intentions to explain about Darren and not to involve Jon in my messed-up life, here it was Thursday morning and I was dressed and ready to begin my day (notice, I did not say "date") with Jonathan Prince. I was not only eager to have a good time, I was desperate to have one.

From the minute I woke up, I'd been working myself into a panic trying not to worry. Was I making a big mistake—or not? Go . . . ? Don't go . . . ? Go . . . ! I'd been wringing my hands with indecision for hours. Now I paced up and down the entry like a condemned man while I waited for Jon to arrive. It was almost anticlimactic when he finally came at ten o'clock.

I think I smiled too much when I introduced Jon to my parents. I know I said a lot of dumb things. I tried to compliment him by telling my parents how intelligent he was and how well he did in school, and I ended up calling him a grinder. I couldn't believe I'd actually said that. I wanted to disappear. I was acting like a teeny-bopper on her first date. Not a date! Forget I said that.

Jon didn't seem to mind, though. He just explained what being a grinder meant at our school, and said he was proud to be one. He even told my dad about his plans to become a marine biologist.

Dad winked at me behind Jon's back, and I was worried he'd come right out and say he liked this one a lot better than Darren.

Mom offered Jon a cup of coffee, tea, hot chocolate, a bran muffin, a toasted bagel, a danish—everything but waffles and sausages. I knew Mom was just trying to be a good hostess, but she was acting a little too eager to suit me. Did my parents really like Jon that much? Or did they just dislike Darren so much more?

"Your parents are nice," Jon said as we were walking to his truck. "You can't help but like them."

"I'm glad. I know they liked you, too." I was still so nervous, I stared at the ground and concentrated on not tripping over any of the cracks in the pavement.

"Good. I wanted them to," he replied honestly.

I looked up into his friendly grin. Jon's deep-blue eyes twinkled at me from under his thick lashes. He didn't just smile with his mouth. When the corners turned up in a smile, his whole face went with it. I wondered if he was always so candid, saying exactly what he felt and thought. I never knew for sure what Darren had on his mind. His smiles did more to conceal his feelings than to express them.

"Where are we going?" I asked after we'd driven for a few minutes. "Is it a secret?"

"No. More in the nature of a surprise. Look out the back window into the bed of the truck, then take a guess."

I looked, but all I saw was a big lump under a black plastic tarp held down by some rocks. "You've brought Clyde along, but you've hidden him under the tarp so you don't get a ticket."

"A ticket for what?"

"Lion-napping, of course. Crossing over the yellow line with a yellow lion?"

Jon groaned. He gave me a raised-eyebrow glare. "Now I know you're lion. You can't get a ticket for that."

We laughed at our own stupid jokes.

"I have no idea what you've got back there," I admitted. "Or where we're going. Do I get any hints?"

"Let me think. . . . Okay . . . laundry detergent and

swimming holes.'' His lips turned up and his eyes crinkled at the corners.

''You can't be serious. What kind of clues are those?'' I stared at his profile, but this time he didn't crack a smile or offer another clue. ''You are serious.''

''We have a long ride ahead of us. Plenty of time for you to figure out where I'm taking you. When you've guessed where we're going, I'll tell you what's in the back of the truck.'' He grinned again, mischievously.

Jon was easy to talk to. Every now and then, during our conversation, I'd make another ridiculous guess but he'd shake his head. ''Nope. Not there either,'' he kept repeating until I wanted to strangle him.

''Disneyland!'' I shouted when I recognized the San Diego Freeway. It was the one place, besides San Diego, I knew the 405 freeway went.

''Great guess . . . but wrong,'' he teased.

''San Diego? Mexico? Central America?''

''Not that long a ride. And that's your last clue.''

''Marineland?'' I asked absentmindedly when we passed a billboard advertising it.

He didn't answer. Not even a no. By accident, I'd finally guessed the right place.

''That's it, isn't it? We're going to Marineland.'' I clapped my hands. I dared him to deny it.

He smiled.

I knew it. I was right!

''You're very close . . . and that's definitely the very last clue I'm going to give you. From now on it's only yes—or no. Oh. By the way, Freddie, Marineland is a no.''

''No?''

''Yup. . . . No. Do you give up?''

''No, I don't give up. I was close, right?'' Now I wanted to guess correctly more than anything. Playing this silly game with Jon was fun. I wanted to figure out the answer and impress him with my overwhelming intelligence. So far, he didn't seem too impressed.

"You're not that close yet . . . but Marineland is. Now, don't make me keep giving you clues. Do you hear? You have to do this on your own or it won't count." He pretended to scowl as we exited the freeway.

"I don't need any help. I can do it alone, Jonathan Prince. Keep your old clues. Now let me see. . . . Laundry detergent is . . . washing powder, and washing powder is . . . soap, and soap is . . . Oh, phooey. I don't get it," I groaned.

Nothing even looked familiar. I had no idea where we were.

"Give up?" He gloated.

"Never! Swimming holes, huh? Like . . . lakes, or ponds, or a pool." I wracked my brain to make sense of the clues. "Soap for a washing machine? Oxydol. Cheer. Ivory Snow. Tide."

"You better give up. You'll never guess it." He had such an innocent look on his face, he looked guilty. He couldn't face me without smiling. "Come on. Say you give up."

I had to be getting close. He sounded a tiny bit worried. "No way. I'm on to something. I know it." I tried to think.

Jon started to whistle.

I looked for a street sign, but there didn't seem to be one.

"Whistle all you want, Jonathan Prince. I know I'm close now. Oxydol and lakes. Ivory Snow and lakes. Tide and lakes." I closed my eyes and concentrated hard.

Jon whistled louder.

I had to be close now. I kept my eyes tightly shut. Think, Freddie, think. Hurry up and guess it. Where was Jon going?

I felt the truck turn right, then left, then right again. I opened one eye for a quick peek. Nothing. Only houses. Lots of big pretty houses.

"Soap and water, soap and water," I kept repeating softly, over and over to myself.

Jon's whistling filled the truck.

"Tide and lakes. Tide and ponds?"

The high-pitched whistle became a shrill squeak.

I was getting excited now. "Tide . . . and . . ."

"We're almost there," Jon warned.

"Of course! Tidepools!" I opened my eyes just as Jon pulled the old truck off the road and stopped the motor.

We were parked on a cliff overlooking the glorious blue Pacific Ocean. Foam-tipped waves rolled landward over the glistening, diamond-sparkled sea to be dashed to smithereens on the rocks below us. Through the open truck windows wafted the smell of salt air, crisp and clean, almost too pure to breathe.

I inhaled deeply, letting my eyes drink in the panorama before me. "Beautiful. I should have known." I leaned back in the seat with a sigh.

"You know, you missed about a dozen different clues. We even passed a huge sign advertising the Tidepool Motel. You were so busy guessing where we were going, you forgot to watch." Jon rested his head on the back of the seat. He looked genuinely happy that his choice had pleased me. For a few minutes we just sat there, smiling at each other.

"Come on. Let's get this show on the road," he said, taking the keys from the ignition and opening the door.

"We're in Palos Verdes, aren't we?" I asked through the open window. "I've never been here before."

He nodded. "Malaga Cove has some of the best tidepools in Southern California, maybe even the world. I love poking around in them. There's a wonderful world to explore in each pool."

Jon's enthusiasm was contagious. I was eager to see his

cove and its marine wonders. "Then what are we waiting for? I want to do some tidepool poking, too."

"And after we explore the pools, we're going to have a picnic on the beach. I made the lunch myself." He helped me out of the cab and we unloaded a wicker picnic basket and a large canvas duffel bag from under the tarp.

"A picnic. Another super surprise," I exclaimed.

"Don't be so sure. I did all the cooking myself—without my mom's help. Surviving this picnic may be your biggest surprise yet."

I laughed—until Jon handed me the oversized duffel to lug down the winding dirt path to the water.

When we reached the sand, we took off our tennis shoes and socks and rolled up our pant legs. Then we spread out an old army blanket Jon took from the duffel. I gathered up his shoes and mine to weight down the corners of the thin blanket.

"You don't need the shoes, Freddie. Just use the rocks."

"What rocks?" I asked.

"The rocks that held down the tarp in the back of the truck. I put them in the duffel bag."

"You did what? You put rocks in the duffel bag *I* had to carry down here? Why you . . ." I leaped across the blanket brandishing a tennis shoe.

Jon ran and I chased him until there was no more air left in my lungs. Winded and gasping, we finally made our way back to the blanket and collapsed.

"That was a dirty trick," I said, still panting.

"You didn't expect me to carry those big rocks, did you? Besides, the basket was twice as heavy as the duffel bag."

"I'll bet," I said and tried to punch him in the arm. He rolled away and I ended up on my face. "I'm too tired to beat you up now. I'll wait and do it later."

"I'll be here," he promised, getting to his feet. "The tidepools await. Let's get a move on." He reached out his hand and in one tug pulled me to my feet.

Side by side we walked along the beach toward the rocks, dodging the waves and scaling the shifting sand dunes. We were all alone on the beach. The cove was deserted.

"Robinson Crusoe in paradise." I sighed, taking in the splendor of the warm sand and blue-green sea and crystal-clear sky.

"And I, your man Thursday, am at your service." Jon made a flourishing bow. "May I present for your enjoyment and edification, Master, your first tidepool." He clambered over some low rocks and I followed.

I gazed transfixed into the little saltwater pond formed by the sheltering rocks and high tides. This was the first time I'd ever seen a real live tidepool close up. I felt as eager as a little kid as I discovered the strange-looking things inside. "What is that?" I asked, pointing to a round purple porcupine.

"A sea urchin."

"It looks dangerous."

"Camouflage, to protect it from giant sushi eaters."

"People eat those things?"

"Only the inside, not the spines. Most of the things from the sea are edible. Someday we will farm the ocean like we do the land to feed the hungry people of the world. One day, whole nations will sustain their populations on crops from the sea. Sea farming is already a fact."

"Is that what you want to do when you're a marine biologist? Be a saltwater farmer in the middle of some vast ocean?"

"That's one of the things."

I looked back into the pool. The urchin didn't look too bad, but raising chickens seemed easier.

"Here, Freddie. Look at these. A cluster of *Caprella californica*."

"California Cinderella?"

"Skeleton shrimp." He swished his hand in the water to give me a better view.

I poked my finger into the cluster of minute shrimp. They were only about one-quarter of an inch long. "You call these shrimp? They're shrimpy all right. How do they taste deep fried?"

"Very tasty, I'm sure. But today, why don't we eat them raw?" Jon teased.

"Yuck. Not me." I moved to another pool. "What's this one?" I called.

"The rest of our lunch," Jon threatened. "That's a *Molpadia arenicola*."

"Yum, yum. I prefer strawberry cola." I dropped a small stone in the pool, but the *Molpadia arenicola* ignored it.

"Actually, in English that's called a sweet potato cucumber. Want a bite?"

"Sounds delicious, but I'll stick to the regular supermarket variety."

Jon picked up the yellowish-green creature—it looked like a two-and-one-half-inch-long skinless cucumber—and held it out. It squirted water at me. "Oh. I forgot to mention, this thing is also called a sea squirt."

"For obvious reasons, I'm sure." I looked down at the dark, wet spot on my sweat shirt.

Jon laughed and put the sea cucumber back into its pool.

We moved from pool to pool, peering into each one while Jon explained the creatures that lived there. Then we trudged the length of the sandy beach, scouring it for pretty shells and rocks that the ocean had worn smooth or into interesting shapes. I filled the pockets of my old jeans, and when they wouldn't hold any more treasures, I filled Jon's pockets, too.

Then I found the cutest little crab skittering sideways along the sand, and immediately fell in love with it. I wanted to keep it, but Jon explained that the sea creatures were protected by law.

"Taking any living thing off this beach without a special license could get you up to a five-thousand-dollar fine," he warned.

"I'll stick to rocks and shells," I assured him, putting the cute little crab back on his rocky ledge. "Bye-bye, you sweet thing," I said and hurried away, dragging Jon behind me.

We kept searching the beach until our stomachs actually growled loud enough to be heard over the crashing waves. We were having so much fun we completely lost track of time. I was grateful when Jon suggested we go back to the blanket and have our picnic.

"I'm totally starved," I announced, flopping down on the blanket.

"Watch the sand. This stuff is going to taste bad enough without adding grit to it," Jon joked.

He handed me things from the basket and I helped spread them out on the checkered cloth he'd put over the old gray army blanket. I laid out paper plates and cups and plastic silverware and napkins.

Jon hadn't forgotten a thing. Everything he took out of the picnic basket looked delicious.

"Did you really make all this yourself? Even the pasta salad?" I asked.

I thought of the times Darren had come over to watch TV with me. He'd sit in front of the set, while I'd whip us up a snack. He was less than useless in the kitchen. I'd truly believed that my dad was the only man in the world who actually knew how to cook anything. Jonathan Prince was looking better all the time.

"Mom taught me to cook. For her own survival, as well as mine. After my dad died, she had to go to work. She took over Prince Plumbing, my dad's plumbing business. She even went back to school and got her plumber's license. Susan Prince has become one first-rate pipe banger. Our company specializes in new housing developments."

"Your mother's a plumber?" I took a big bite of the pasta salad. "Ummm. Chicken. This is delicious."

"Thanks. And she runs the company, too. She's president of Prince-S Plumbing—that's what Mom renamed it—as well as one of the fitters. I'm really proud of her."

"Boy, I don't blame you. She sounds like a wonder." I bit into a roll and accepted the cold glass of lemonade Jon poured for me. I eyed the chocolatey brownies peeking out of their covered dish, and my mouth watered. When Jon got married, he was going to make some lady very happy with his extraordinary culinary skills.

"You're right. Mom's definitely a wonder woman. But Prince-S Plumbing is still small, and there's not a lot of spendable cash yet. As much of the profits as we can spare go back into the business to help it grow. Mom works hard, I go to school, we both cook and clean. It's a good system." He talked between swallows, but I nodded and kept right on eating. "It takes both of us to make it work," he added.

"But you work and go to school, too. Where do you find the time? Doesn't so much responsibility ever get to you?"

Jon thought for a minute.

I think I already knew his answer. I envied the satisfied look on his face. You could tell he felt good about helping out at home. I thought about my family. How much Mom and Dad have had to sacrifice, and how hard they worked to see we had a good life. I thought about my contribution and wondered if I was doing my share to help. My working to earn my own money for Winterfest had to help a little. But I was going to try to do more. Mom and Dad deserved it.

We finished eating and put away the leftovers, wrapping up the soiled utensils. Jon's lunch had been great. And conversation came so easily, time seemed to speed by. I didn't want the afternoon to end. I was having too much fun. I kept thinking I should feel guilty for enjoying myself so much with Jon, but I didn't. I felt happy.

Finally, Jon answered. "I don't party much. My spare time usually goes into studying. I guess there are times when school and work and money problems do get me down a little. But I get over it. Mom's great to me. I have a few really good friends. I do get to go scuba diving once in a while; I use my dad's old equipment. I guess I've got a lot to be happy about. More, every single day. And I think I've got a pretty bright future ahead of me, too. Someday I'm going to repay my mom for everything she's done for me."

What a neat person he is, I thought. I looked at Jon and smiled. There really wasn't anything that needed saying.

This time I carried the almost empty picnic basket up the hill, and Jon hefted the duffel bag with the rocks. As we walked along the path together, and I listened to Jon tell about life after his dad had died, it suddenly occurred to me that I'd never known a boy as sensitive as Jon in my whole life.

I'd had a few boyfriends, and been friends with a lot more in junior high and high school in Camden. I'd known lots of guys who were better-looking, funnier, more athletic, and certainly more popular than Jon. In fact, Darren was all of those things. But Darren wasn't sensitive or caring. Not in the same way Jon was. Comparisons between Jon and Darren raced around inside my head, bumping into one another. My thoughts confused me.

I sat next to Jon, feeling comfortable and relaxed, as he drove me home. We were like old friends, talking and laughing and sharing past experiences we'd had.

Jon told me about his love for the ocean, and about snorkeling and scuba diving and fishing underwater with a spear. I was pretty impressed.

Then we talked about Sammy and Birdie and Noah. Jon told me all the crazy stories that had happened during his first two years working at the Funny Farm before I got there.

He was so funny, and we were having such a good time, I wanted the drive home to last forever. I never wanted to stop talking and laughing with Jon.

Over and over, the same terrible thoughts kept coming back: Was Darren really worth it? Was he so special, so wonderful? What did I feel for Darren right now, sitting beside Jon, besides a ton of guilt for having such a good time?

If it was guilt I wanted, then I should have been thrilled when Jon walked me to my door and said good-bye.

"Thanks for spending the day with me, Freddie. I had a great time."

"Me too, Jon. Everything was really nice. Especially your lunch."

He blushed. It made him look so vulnerable, I had to smile.

"I'll see you tomorow at school. . . ." He hesitated, looking deeply into my eyes.

"And at the Funny Farm." I stared back.

I felt drawn to him. I could feel my body swaying toward him. I wanted Jon to kiss me!

"Oh, sure. There, too," he choked out. Then he turned and ran for his truck.

I was drowning in guilt. Guilt! Guilt! Guilt!

Or was it disappointment?

Chapter Ten

"FREDDIE. TELEPHONE," Dad called from the family room.

"I have to take a bath and wash the sand out of my hair. If that's Barbara, tell her I'll call her back after I'm done." I stood shivering in my underwear at the top of the stairs. I couldn't talk now. I'd already filled the tub and my water was getting cold.

When Barb and I had spoken on Wednesday night, I'd finally told her that Jon had asked me to spend Thursday with him. She was probably calling to get a blow-by-blow news report. What was I going to tell her? The truth? What was the truth, anyway? Maybe after a good soak in the tub I'd be able to figure it out.

"It's not Barbara. It's Darren," Dad hollered back.

"On my way," I shouted, wrapping a bath towel around me and taking the stairs two at a time.

"What happened to Jon?" Dad asked, as he handed me the phone.

I covered the receiver with my hand. "Nothing happened to Jon. We're just good friends, that's all."

"Good friends, huh?" Dad winked at me like he'd done that morning. "I like your new little friend, kiddo." He gave my bottom a friendly swat then went back to vegetate in front of the TV.

New little friend! Sometimes I wanted to throttle him. Even if he was my dad.

"Darren?" I said into the receiver.

"Yeah. Where were you? I've been waiting forever."

"I was just about to get into the tub. I have to wash my hair."

"To get the sand out. So I heard."

"Huh?"

"Your dad just filled me in. What were you doing going out on a date with that grinder? Are you or aren't you going with me?"

"It wasn't a date. We just went to Palos Verdes to see the tidepools. And I wasn't so sure."

"Sure? About what?"

"If you were still going with me. You seemed to have disappeared lately. I thought that you and Sandi—"

"Well, you thought wrong. Sandi's just a very old friend—and you know it. Look, Freddie. I don't have to make excuses, you know. I've been busy. The Senior Council has had a lot of work to do, planning fund-raisers and things like that. I mean, what are people going to say if they see Darren Gresham's girl out with some social-misfit grinder? Why did you go to the tidepools, anyway? You need the points for biology or something?"

"No. Jon just asked me to go." I knew better than to admit I'd had no idea where we'd be going when I'd accepted Jon's offer. "It was just something to do. Jon's a friend. So I said I'd go."

"Well, you're through going places with him. If we're going together, I don't want you to have wimps for friends."

The mean names Darren was calling Jon made me feel terrible. Jon wasn't any of the things Darren was saying about him. But Darren was only talking that way because he was jealous. I knew he didn't really mean what he was saying. And he was jealous of Jon! He was hurt because I'd gone somewhere with another boy. If I defended Jon now, he'd only get that much more upset. I didn't want to make Darren miserable, not when he was making me feel absolutely wonderful—now that I knew he still loved me. I'd been silly to think Sandi could take him away from me. I was still Darren's girl. Me . . . not Sandi Moses.

"So, how about meeting tomorrow at morning break? In front of my locker. Okay?" Darren wanted me to be in our usual meeting place, at our usual time—nothing had changed.

"Okay. I'll be there, Darren."

"I just may have something important, something special, to ask you when I see you." The tone of Darren's voice had changed. All the anger was gone. "You love me, Freddie?" he asked in a teasing voice.

"You know I do," I answered. We kissed good-bye and hung up.

I do. I do. I do. I went to take my bath.

I sat in my first-period homeroom and listened to the morning bulletin:

> "Because this is Clean Up Our Campus Week, I know you students will be making an extra-special effort to can all your campus trash. And, speaking of things that are extra special, our wonderful senior class will be having its latest

fund-raiser next Sunday at Wildwood Park, in
Encino. The cost will be only two dollars for
swimming, hot dogs, and a hayride. No self-
respecting senior will want to miss this exciting
event—so plan ahead. That's it for the morning bulletin. This is Cherie Maymen signing
off. . . ."

I was in big trouble, and I knew it. That had to be the
special, important thing that Darren wanted to talk to me
about. This was to be a test. To see if I loved him enough to
go to the swim party no matter what. What was I going to do?
I could ask the Holdens for that Sunday off. But if they had to
work . . . What was I going to do?

"What are you going to do?" Barbara asked. She was
walking me over to Darren's locker. "You know what Darren is going to say. If you really loved him . . . etcetera."

"I do love him. It's just that the Holdens are counting on
me. They've got such a tight filming schedule because they
can only use the location Friday nights, Saturdays, and Sundays. If they're filming that Sunday, I'm dead." I looked at
Barbara, who shook her head in sympathy. "I don't know
what I'm going to do."

"With or without you, Freddie, I'll bet Darren is there."

"Come on, Barb. Be fair. Darren has to go. He's the
vice-president of the Senior Council. It's his duty to be
there." I defended Darren, but Barbara wasn't telling me
anything I didn't already know.

"And Sandi is the shadow in charge of the vice-president.
She wants Darren back, Freddie. I think she'll do just about
anything to get him back." Barbara raised her eyebrows
meaningfully. "I love you, Freddie, and I don't want to see
you get hurt. But I think Darren will let Sandi do just about
anything—if you know what I mean."

I knew what she meant. Darren's girlfriends usually did whatever they had to do to keep him. We'd been through that, right at the start of our relationship. I wasn't ready for that, though, and he had always respected my feelings. I wondered, for the millionth time, just how badly Sandi wanted Darren back.

"Hi," Barbara called to Wiz, as we neared Darren's locker. He was standing with Darren and Mason; the three of them were deep in a heated discussion. "What's the debate about?" she asked.

"Nothing important," said Wiz. "Football. The Raiders' chances of making it to the Super Bowl this year."

Wiz loved football, he was an avid Raiders fan.

"Come on. I want to get some hot chocolate," Barbara said, dragging Wiz away. "Football, football, football. . . . Honestly, Ozgood Greenwald, don't you ever get tired of talking about the Raiders?"

"Ahh, Barb," Wiz groaned. But he went with her.

"I gotta meet Sandi," Mason said. "See you guys." He left, too.

"Well?" Darren said.

"Well," I answered.

"Want some chocolate, or something?" He took my hand.

"No, thank you." I shook my head. We stared at each other in silence for a moment. Go on! Say it! My heart thumped inside my chest. Ask me about going to the swimming party, so we can fight some more. "But if you want . . ."

"No. So, listen. I guess you heard the announcement. I wanted to surprise you," Darren said. "Really great, isn't it?"

"I guess so," I answered. "I might have to work. I hope I can go."

"What do you mean, you 'hope'? Look, Freddie. The

swimming party is a week away. You'll just have to tell the people you work for that you're taking the day off. If you won't go with me, I'll find someone who will. You can call in sick or something.''

''I can't do that, Darren. If the Holdens have to work, then so do I. They are depending on me to watch Sammy until they're finished filming their series. I don't have a choice.''

''It sounds to me like you've already made one. Maybe it's not the chimp you're so hung up on, huh? Maybe you just like playing Jane of Jungleland with your wimpy Tarzan. Maybe you're too busy playing games with that grinder to go to the swimming party with me. You know something, Freddie? I don't need this. And I don't need you. I can have any girl at Woodlake I want. I must have been crazy to think I wanted you. I'm through letting a nobody like you make a jerk out of me. I'm Senior Council vice-president!''

''But . . . but . . . Darren!'' I sobbed out his name.

Everyone in the hall turned to stare at me. Tears streamed down my cheeks. I had to look like a total fool, standing hunched against the lockers, crying my eyes out. And I didn't even care what I looked like, or what the other kids thought. I dug into my jacket pocket for a tissue. As usual, I didn't have one. I felt so light-headed and dizzy. I lurched forward and my stomach turned over. I'm going to be sick, I thought. Nose running, eyes streaming, and insides churning, I ran for the bathroom.

I didn't throw up; it was something I rarely did. I think if I had, I'd have felt better. I crawled into one of the stalls, grateful there was no one in the bathroom but me. I sank down onto a closed toilet seat and let my tears flow freely. When the passing bell for my next class shrilled in the empty restroom, my insides jumped but I didn't make an effort to get up. I just sat there, holding my aching middle, and cried. I was afraid to move. I felt too sick and too shaky to go to my next class.

"Freddie? Are you in here?" Barbara's voice came over the partition.

"Yes," I answered weakly.

"Are you all right?"

"No."

"Can I come in?"

"Yes." I unlocked the door.

"I heard what happened. Everybody was whispering about your fight with Darren. I thought you two had made up."

"So did I. Everything was terrific until the subject of the senior swim party came up."

"And you told him that you have to work?" Barbara guessed.

"I don't even know if I do or not. I only said I might have to—if the Holdens needed me, and . . ." My insides did another flip and I moaned in pain.

"And Darren went off the deep end. Maybe it isn't any of my business, and maybe I shouldn't say anything, but I dated the great man once, too. Take it from one of Darren Gresham's ex-doormats, Freddie, he isn't worth it. He goes into every relationship for what he can get out of it. You were new at Woodlake when he met you. You looked up to him, fed his ego, followed him around like a grateful puppy. He doesn't like it now that you have a life and a mind of your own. You don't need him. He needs you, Freddie. And he needs you to need him. . . . Does that make any sense?"

"Yes. I guess so. But I love him, Barb."

"You love Darren? Or what Darren is? Are you sure it isn't the handsome, popular, and enviable VP of the Senior Council you love?" Barbara looked me straight in the eyes without blinking. Her honesty was unnerving.

I felt like a laser beam was searing into my brain, forcing me to look into the hole it burned through to my thoughts. I didn't know what to answer. Was it Darren I loved? Or did I love being part of his group? Did I love knowing that every girl in school envied me my boyfriend and wanted to be me? Was I afraid of losing Darren's love, or the status it gave me? As long as I had him I was "in." I was special. I was Darren's girl. Without him I would be just another lost soul. One of the hundreds of other sad and lonely girls without a boyfriend's love to protect them from being unwanted and alone.

Barbara's gaze didn't waver.

"When we're together, Barb, when he kisses me, I come unglued. I must love him. I never felt that way when I kissed guys back in Ohio."

"How old were you, back in Ohio? Thirteen? Fourteen? Big deal. Baby kisses. Darren's a master, Freddie. He's had a lot of practice—take my word for it. When I went out with him and he kissed me, I came unglued, too. But not nearly as unglued as I get when Wiz kisses me. Next to Wiz, Darren Gresham's not even a 'has-been,' he's a 'never-was.' Besides, look at poor Sandi. . . . You want to be like her? She's still unglued over him."

"I don't know. . . ."

"Then find out. Kiss someone else. There are plenty of guys who would kill to date you—let alone kiss you, you dodo." Barbara's voice echoed off the porcelain walls in the green-tiled bathroom. "Dodo—dodo—dodo."

"Oh, sure. They're lining up." I stood up. "Name me five. Three. Two. Name me one."

Barbara backed out of the stall. "Jon Prince, for one. You went out on a date with him. Don't tell me he doesn't like you. Did he kiss you?"

"Barbara! No, he didn't kiss me."

"You sound disappointed."

"Barbara, please! We didn't go out—exactly. It wasn't like a date. I keep telling you that. We're friends. We work at the same place. I'm probably the only girl he's not afraid to be with. He's a grinder—remember?"

"You keep telling yourself that if it makes you feel better about having a *date* with him. But don't expect Jon to think it wasn't a date. I'll bet he has a completely different idea about it."

I was about to argue the fine points of actually dating someone versus spending the day with him, when the five-minute passing bell for the next class vibrated through the empty bathroom. In less than a minute the room began to fill with masses of chattering, giggling girls. They filled the stalls and a line was quickly formed behind the rows of hand washers and mirror gazers. It was impossible to move without bumping into someone who wanted to fill the same exact spot you occupied.

"Do you feel better now? Are you ready to face the world?" Barbara grabbed my arm and ripped me out of the path of a four-person collision.

I hugged her. "Yes, thank you."

We wove between more females trying to squeeze into the already jammed restroom and pushed toward the doors.

"Then let's get out of here," Barbara yelled over her shoulder, pressing forward. "While we still can."

I followed in her wake.

We didn't speak until we reached the door to the gym, our next class. Then Barbara took my hand and pulled me to a stop.

"You're not mad at me, are you? For what I said about Darren?"

"Don't be silly. We're friends."

"Best friends. I don't like to see you hurting."

"I know that. Thanks. I'm not mad. Honestly, I'm not."

"Okay. I believe you. But promise me you won't get mad at what I'm going to say now." She looked so worried and serious. She was my best friend; she really cared.

I smiled. "I promise."

"You work tomorrow, don't you?"

"Yes. I work every Saturday."

"Does Jon work, too?"

"I suppose so. So far he's been there every day that I've been there."

"Then make an effort. Okay?"

"An effort?"

"Show Jon you're available. Let him know you think he's nice. Give Jon a chance. You won't be sorry. You don't need Darren Gresham. Will you do it?"

"I don't know if I can. I still feel like I'm Darren's girl. Barbara, I don't even know how to flirt."

"You can learn. Just try, okay? Please, Freddie. Will you?"

"I'll try," I promised.

Try what? I wondered. I'd never come on to a guy before in my life. That was a Sandi Moses specialty. How was I supposed to let Jon know I was "available"? Was I? Were Darren and I really through? For good?

Would Jon even care?

Chapter Eleven

THE ENTIRE TIME I fed Sammy, waited for him to wake up from his nap, got him dressed, and carefully hooked him into his stroller for his walk, I kept telling myself the same dumb story. I wasn't nervous and I wasn't anxious. I wasn't doing this because of what Barbara had said. I wasn't going to the compound just to see Jon. Personally, I couldn't have cared less about taking a walk. I wasn't doing this for me. I was doing it all for Sammy—so he could visit with his friend. I was only going along for the ride—someone had to push the stroller, right? My only concern was for Sammy. He needed the fresh air. That's what I kept telling myself. I also pretended I believed it.

"Sit down in that stroller, Sammy. Right now, or else."

He may not have understood the words, but he understood the tone of voice. With an exasperated sigh, Sammy flopped into the stroller and waited.

I made a big show of acting unhurried. I cut up two apples into wedges and peeled an orange, tearing it into sections before dropping Sammy's gourmet snack into a plastic bag,

then securing it with a loose knot at the top. Then I slipped on
my sweater, tied the hood of Sammy's jacket under his chin,
and proceeded to move toward the front door in slow motion.
Any minute I expected to break into loud choruses of "I
Don't Care, I Don't Care."

As always, when he realized we were headed for the
compound and Jon, Sammy began to screech, thump the tray
of his stroller, and in general announce loudly that we were
on our way. And, as usual, Jon heard us coming and was
waiting by the path to the snake house.

"Hi, you two. I was wondering if you were planning on
making the rounds today." He moved toward us, his boots
scraping on the gravel.

Jon looked like a cowboy in his boots, old blue work shirt,
and well-worn jeans. The straw Stetson and the red print scarf
he'd tied around his neck looked nice on him. He didn't look
the least little bit like Tarzan of the Apes, I thought, remembering what Darren had called us.

Jon was no Tarzan, and I wasn't Jane, either. I tried to
imagine him in a leopard skin, beating his chest and swinging
around the compound from vine to vine. I pictured Sammy
and me swinging along after him, yelling, "Wait for us,
Tarzan! Wait for us!" My mental images made me giggle.
Jon might look good in a skimpy loincloth, but the swinging
part and Sammy and me . . . well, that part did seem awfully
farfetched. Except . . . the way the front of his hair stood
up, cut short but still silky-looking, was kind of carefree and
wild. Ridiculous. Tarzan had long hair, and Jon's hair was
short in the back, neatly trimmed. There was absolutely no
resemblance.

Without unhooking the leash, Jon stooped down and lifted
Sammy onto his knee. "How ya' doin', little fella?" he
crooned.

Sammy hugged him tightly and chattered into his ear.

"It was boring being stuck in the house. The weather is just too nice," I said, to justify my being there.

"I'm glad you came down. I was hoping you would."

"You were?" Was Barbara right about him? Did Jon think we'd had a date, too?

"Uh-huh. There's something special I want you to see." He led the way down the path away from the snake house.

"Another surprise?" Why had I said that? Was it a test? To see if he remembered Thursday?

"Kind of. But this isn't like my pasta salad; you can't eat this one." He did remember. For some reason that made me extremely happy.

Sammy must have sensed we were going to see something special; he suddenly started acting really hyper. He held on to the bar around the front of his stroller and bounced up and down on the seat. Too much of that and Birdie would need to buy him a new stroller for his walks. I didn't jump up and down, but I was excited to see Jon's surprise, too.

"Shush, Sammy," Jon coaxed, patting the chimp to calm him. "We have to be quiet now." He picked up his boots and put them down more carefully, trying to make as little noise as possible.

"Is it an animal?" I asked. "Is something asleep?"

"In there." Jon stopped several feet away from an enclosure. "And it's two animals. They ran around like wild Indians all day, until they finally collapsed. Now they're sleeping it off so they can go at it again."

I looked inside. A female lion was curled protectively around two cubs. She licked their bodies and faces while they slept. "Ohhh," I sighed. "How adorable."

"The mama's name is Clover. Her twins are Caesar and Cleopatra. And the proud papa is—"

"Let me guess. Clyde, the king of beasts, the lord of the jungle, who sells raincoats on prime-time TV?" I oohed and ahhed and couldn't take my eyes off of the precious little lions. They looked like overgrown kittens. I could see why Clyde would be proud.

"They're Clyde's offspring," Jon said. "But he's not king or lord of anything since he met Clover. She wears the pants in their family."

I giggled. "Smart lady. Is she a good mama?"

"The best. She keeps those little troublemakers so clean, she just about licks the fur off of them."

Clover seemed to know we were talking about her babies. She glanced over at us and threw back her head proudly. Then, to show us how little our opinions mattered to her, she yawned and went back to licking her cubs.

"I love them. I wish I could hug those sweet things to pieces," I said. I rocked Sammy's stroller to keep him from disturbing the sleeping babies.

"She'd never allow it," said Jon. "You've heard of the ferocity of a lioness protecting her cubs. Don't let Clover's sweet pussycat face fool you, she'd never let you get close enough for a hug." Jon made what he must have thought was a ferocious face and snarled at me.

I laughed and pretended to cower and shake. "I didn't say I was going to. I'm not crazy, you know."

"I am," Jon said. He growled at me again. Then his voice grew serious. "You bring out the beast in me. But I'd let you get close enough for a hug."

"You would?" Was Barbara right, after all?

"Freddie?"

"Yes." I held my breath. I had that same feeling. The one I'd had when we'd said good-bye on Thursday. I felt like I was being drawn to him. Like I wanted him to . . .

"I . . . um . . . Freddie?"

"Yes, Jon."

"Yes?"

"Yes. . . ."

Then he kissed me. His mouth was soft and sweet and so gentle. And I felt like I was falling apart. Just like Barbara had promised, I was coming unglued. I put my arms around his neck and kissed him back. My thoughts roared in my head. Then I realized my thoughts weren't roaring—Clover was.

Sammy shrieked back at Clover, turning over his stroller.

I broke away from Jon, laughing self-consciously.

Jon lifted Sammy up and untangled his leash from the stroller wheels. "I'll carry him for a while," he offered.

Sammy wrapped his arms around Jon's neck and his legs around his waist and snuggled his head into Jon's shoulder.

I pushed the empty stroller and followed them. My heart had stopped pounding and I was breathing normally again, but that was the only part of me that felt normal. I couldn't believe what had just happened. Jon had kissed me. I had kissed him back—and I'd liked it. I'd liked it so much, I wanted him to kiss me again.

The path away from Clover and her babies had a slight rise. At the top, on a grassy patch, stood a tall, leafy, fruitless mulberry tree. Jon sat down and shifted Sammy onto his lap. He looked up at me questioningly.

I hesitated for a second then dropped down beside them.

We just sat there, neither one of us saying a word for the longest time. Not even the bees buzzing or the leaves rustling disturbed the feeling of utter stillness that surrounded us.

Jon finally spoke. His voice seemed to explode in the silence. His words came so unexpectedly they made me jump.

"I'm sorry, Freddie. I shouldn't have done that. I have no right to kiss you. I know you're going with Darren."

"It wasn't your fault, Jon. I'm to blame as much as you are. Please, just forget it. It doesn't matter." I pulled up a blade of dark-green grass and wound it around my little finger.

"I guess it doesn't. Not to you." He sounded hurt.

I hadn't meant to hurt him. I liked Jon—a lot. But I didn't want him to let one kiss end the friendship that was beginning to grow between us. I especially didn't want him to feel bad—or guilty—because of me.

On the other hand, that was exactly how I was feeling— loaded with guilt. I was very glad Jon had kissed me. I'd wanted him to do it. And now, I wanted to tell him how much his kiss did matter to me; only I didn't dare say anything.

"I guess I'm pretty stupid. A grinder who thinks he has a chance with one of the prettiest girls in school. I know how it is with you and Darren Gresham; you're his girl. Brother, what a jerk you must think I am."

"I don't think anything of the sort, Jon."

Sammy had crawled off Jon's lap and was trying to shinny up the tree. I stood up and pulled him down. He walked to the end of his leash and sat down with his back to us.

"He'll probably eat those weeds he's playing with," Jon said, reeling in the leash.

"I have something he'll like better than weeds." I went to the stroller and took the plastic bag from the basket. "I brought these along for a snack."

Sammy saw the bag and did a somersault, clapping his hands and chirping his excitement.

"Whatever you have in there, he must love it," Jon said.

"Nothing special, an orange and some apple wedges."

"Chimp food. My favorite. Think Sammy will share with a friend?"

I looked at Jon. "I would love to share my half with a friend." I tried to emphasize the word *friend*.

Jon smiled at last. "Let's eat, Sammy," he called, pulling the rambunctious ape back into his lap.

We took turns handing chunks of apples and orange sections to Sammy, putting every other piece into our own mouths.

Sammy's method of consuming oranges included squishing them between his fingers before chewing. It was wet and sticky sitting next to him while he mutilated his treat.

One good thing about Sammy's antics, they successfully changed the subject and lightened our mood. Both Jon and I acted as if nothing unusual had happened all day. We munched fruit, played games, and made silly faces with Sammy. We discussed the baby lions and the mother lion and the father lion. And we pretended (at least I was pretending) to have forgotten all about the kiss we'd shared.

"I'll walk you back to the house," Jon offered. "I better get back on the job. I still have some work to finish." He put Sammy back into the stroller and secured the leash to the safety ring attached to the seat.

Sammy resisted and screeched in anger. He wasn't ready to stop playing.

"I'd like to roll around on the grass and play with you all day, but duty calls." Jon spoke to Sammy, but I caught him looking at me from under the cover of his lashes.

A funny twinge grabbed me, just under my ribs. I felt breathless for a second.

Why was I letting Jon affect me like this? Yesterday it was Darren. Today it was Jon. Was I really that fickle? Or was I just flattered? I know I liked the way Jon chose to flatter me.

Be careful, my brain warned me. Your ego has been in the pits lately. You just need to feel good about yourself, that's all. You're reading more into one little kiss than there really is. Get hold of yourself, I warned.

"Are you taking time off to go to the senior swim party?" Jon asked. If he'd been hoping for a neutral subject we could discuss, he should have picked something else.

"I can't," I said, wishing I could think of something else to politely change the subject to. "I asked Birdie for the day off. But they're on call every Saturday and Sunday for the next two weeks. I'll have to be with Sammy."

"That's too bad."

"You going?" I knew Jon's job didn't depend on the Holdens' work schedule. As long as he got his work done, he could take time off from the compound if he wanted to.

"No. I'm not going, either," he answered offhandedly. Obviously, he didn't want to go.

"Jon, you're wasting your whole senior year. You never do anything with the rest of the class." I wished I had his job instead of mine. I'd know how to take advantage of his flexible hours.

"I don't want to do anything with the rest of our class. I don't even know most of the kids in it. None of my good friends will be at the swim party. We don't go to those kinds of things."

"You could know all the kids," I insisted. "Not just the smart ones, but the fun ones, too. You've gone to school with most of them all your life. You just don't want to be friendly. Isolating yourself is really dumb."

I found myself getting angry at having to point this out to Jon. And he was making me feel like a pompous fool. Who was I to be giving anyone lectures on appropriate social behavior? If Barbara hadn't befriended me, I'd still be wandering around Woodlake alone.

"I don't isolate myself. I just have better things to do than be an empty-headed social butterfly. If being accepted and having 'fun' friends means being a hanger-on in the popular crowd, no thank you, that doesn't appeal to me. I wouldn't do it—not for anyone!" He was almost yelling at me. What had I done?

"Is that what you think I am?" I raised my voice, too. "An

empty-headed butterfly? An 'in' crowd hanger-on?" How dare he insinuate such a thing! How dare a grinder talk to me like that!

"Aren't you, Freddie? You follow around after Darren and Sandi Moses and that whole bunch. Name me one unsocial thing that has ever occupied one second of their time."

"You don't even know my friend Barbara, or her boyfriend, Wiz. And Darren is the vice-president of Senior Council, Jon. That comes under the heading of class service."

"Sure. He's VP in charge of partying. A buddy of mine is on the council—a lowly worker. He says that Darren only shows up to vote on the next good time. Wake up, Freddie. There is more to life than having fun."

"You wake up, Jonathan Prince. Studying and working all the time is very noble, but it's turning you into a . . . a . . . nerdy gorilla. Now give me my monkey and leave me alone."

"Ape," Jon corrected.

"Who cares." I yanked the stroller out of his hand and ran the rest of the way to the ranch house awkwardly pushing it in front of me.

At the porch, I unhooked Sammy and ran up the stairs. I was about to shut the front door behind me when something made me turn.

"I just want to be sure *he* isn't following me," I hissed to Sammy.

The path was empty. Jon was gone. I slammed the door shut with all my might.

Chapter Twelve

I GUESS IF I hadn't been so mad at Jon for what he'd said about my friends, I'd never have spoken to Darren or Sandi again. Well, maybe I would have spoken to Darren, but not Sandi, that's for sure. I just didn't like having my choice of friends ridiculed, even the ones I didn't like very much.

Sandi probably had a lot of good qualities; I'd simply been too preoccupied with her bad ones to notice.

Darren wasn't at all the way Jon described him. He did a lot of worthwhile things on the Senior Council. He was always telling me about some project or other the council was planning.

Jon didn't even know my best friend, but he'd gone right ahead and lumped her in there with the rest of us empty-headed social butterflies. Barbara, on the other hand, had only the nicest things to say about him. That made his cutting her down worse than anything else.

Barbara was a sweet person and a wonderful friend. She and Wiz were probably the two neatest people in Woodlake High School. They were absolutely the nicest people I knew.

I'd do anything for Barb, if she asked me.

That's why, when Wiz's mother, Mrs. Greenwald, invited Barbara over to her house to learn how to bake *mandelbroit*, a delicious Jewish cookie, and told Barbara she should bring all her girlfriends, I said I'd go, too.

When Barbara asked me, she didn't pull any punches. She came right out and said that Sandi and her shadow, Janet, were going, too. She said if I didn't think I could handle being around Sandi, she'd understand.

I knew Barb meant it, but she looked so disappointed just talking about my not coming along, I knew I had to go. So I said yes, I wouldn't miss a once-in-a-lifetime opportunity to learn to make Mrs. Greenwald's wonderful *mandelbroit*. I even promised I'd talk nice to Sandi and be on my best behavior.

"I'm nervous about seeing Darren; I don't know what to say," I admitted in a whisper. Barbara and I were standing together, several feet away from Sandi and Janet. We were sprinkling cinnamon and cutting the long rolls of dough into half-moons before putting them into the oven.

"Just be yourself," Barbara advised. "Don't worry about Darren. He must have asked me twenty times if you were going to be here. I know he wants to see you. After a whole week of Sandi, he couldn't help but realize what a good thing he gave up." She laughed softly.

I laughed, too, but I wasn't so sure.

In twenty minutes basketball practice would be over. Then all the guys were coming over to Wiz's house to taste the fruits of our baking labors. It'd be the first time Darren and I would be together in the same room in days. We hadn't said more than two words to each other in over a week. And none of those words had been particularly private. Sandi had always been there. Find Darren and you found Sandi, too. She'd never been more than a few feet away from him all week.

My argument with Jon had done a lot to make me doubt
myself. My behavior with him had been terrible. He wasn't
entirely to blame for the kiss we'd shared. I was embarrassed
by how much I'd wanted Jon to kiss me, and by my eager
response. On that score, I was totally to blame. But I couldn't
forgive his hateful words about my friends and me. The
things he'd said were absolutely unforgivable.

Still, what had happened with Jon wasn't all bad. It had
made me stop and think and begin to take stock of my
faltering relationship with Darren. It had forced me to recon-
sider Darren's actions and his attitudes. Just maybe he wasn't
as selfish as I'd been telling myself. Now, instead of blaming
him for being so demanding, I began to wonder if I hadn't let
him down a lot, too. We were supposed to be going together.
Except we weren't going anywhere he wanted to go. It was a
well-known fact that it took two people to be a couple. How
could we be a couple if I was always working? I'd wanted the
best senior year ever. For me, that meant Darren and Winterfest. But it was Darren's senior year, too. Was it so hard to
understand why he might want to take his steady girl to a few
of his senior class activities? He was the council vice-
president, after all. The idea of going to every event alone
had to upset him. It upset me, too. But had I made that clear to
him? If not, that was what I was going to do as soon as he got
to Wiz's house. We were going to talk and, I hoped, make
up.

The swim party was positively the very last thing Darren
would have to go to without me. The Holdens' TV series
would be on hiatus after next week. That meant no more
weekend filming for a while. They'd asked if I would still sit
for Sammy, but only once in a while in the evenings.

I'd said yes. Not because of the money, either. I had my
three hundred dollars, and more, for my share of Winterfest.
I'd said I'd sit because I liked the Holdens and Sammy and
I wanted to help Birdie and Noah find time to get away

alone. I knew now how important that was to a lasting relationship.

"Hey! Watch what you're doing, Freddie." Barbara held up her cinnamon-sprinkled arm. "This is not *mandelbroit*. This is my arm."

"Sorry. I was thinking about something else. I'll keep my mind on my work from now on. I promise."

Barbara and I carried our second cookie sheet to the oven.

"Barbara, did you get that new bikini you wanted for the swim party?" Sandi asked. "It seems as if every girl I've talked to has bought something new."

"No," Barbara answered. "I didn't have to. Freddie's letting me wear her new lavender suit. It's gorgeous. I love it."

"It looks fantastic on you, too, Barb. Much better than it does on me." I hated to admit it, but I was telling the truth. I'd offered to lend it the minute I knew I wouldn't be going. At first Barbara hadn't wanted to wear it, but I'd convinced her. With her violet eyes, she looked sensational in it—a real knockout. I told her she owed it to Wiz to be the best-looking girl at the party. For Wiz's sake, she'd finally agreed.

"I don't think I remember it," Sandi mused.

"I've never really had a chance to wear it. I bought it on sale at the end of the summer. It was the bikini bargain of the century. That's the one thing about Southern California I'll never understand," I said. "In Ohio it makes sense to have after-summer sales. No one needs a bikini when it's snowing. But it's November and the weather in the Valley is still in the eighties. It's like having Thanksgiving in the middle of August."

"I suppose you have a point," Sandi said. "I never shop at sales."

Look for her finer qualities. Be nice, I reminded myself, as I felt my temperature start to rise. "What kind of bathing suit

are you going to wear? Have we ever seen it?'' There! I'd
forced out something nice even though I couldn't have cared
less what Sandi planned on wearing.

Sandi had so many clothes she probably never had to wear
the same bathing suit twice.

''Her silver. Right, Sandi? I love the silver,'' Janet said.

I remembered the silver suit. It was something you never
forgot. Did I say ''suit''? That was a ludicrous description of
Sandi's silver Band-Aids. Suddenly, all of Sandi's good
qualities flooded into my mind. Her long model's legs, her
delicate waist, her great chest, her flowing blond hair, her
deeply tanned skin (so much exposed, deeply tanned skin!),
and all of it wrapped (but barely) in a silver bikini.

Sandi looked over at me and just smiled.

It was a struggle to remember why I shouldn't just flatten
Sandi with one of the karate chops I'd learned from Sammy.
Why was I even trying to be nice? Sandi sure wasn't.

I was doing it for my best friend. For Barbara. I'd promised her I would be nice, hadn't I? I couldn't embarrass my
best friend in front of her boyfriend's mother, could I? Well,
could I? I was seriously considering it.

''Girls!'' called Mrs. Greenwald from the den. ''I have
bad news.'' She sounded so cheerful I thought she must have
meant to say she had good news.

Sandi, Janet, and I followed Barbara into the den. I was
wrong—it was bad news.

''That was Ozgood on the phone,'' said Mrs. Greenwald.
''He asked me to drive you girls home when we were done
with our *mandelbroit* baking. I'm afraid the boys aren't
coming.''

''Ohhh,'' we all said at once.

''Is something the matter?'' asked Barbara.

''Ozgood said something about Mason's van and a water
hose. I think they're waiting for the automobile club to come

get them. Boys and their cars,'' exclaimed Mrs. Greenwald.
"It's always something."

Now what? I wondered as we cleaned up the mess in the
kitchen and got ready to go home. I'd missed my chance to
talk to Darren before the swim party. What was I going to do
now? I felt miserable.

In the back of my mind was the picture of Sandi, the
silver-clad *femme fatale*. No guy at the senior party without a
girl to guard him and keep him distracted would be safe from
her display. I'd seen the suit; it would take a lot of willpower
to resist it. Without a doubt, Darren would be her main target,
and I wasn't so sure he'd try to resist.

Chapter Thirteen

THE DAY OF THE swim party was beautiful. In the high seventies, the DJ on my clock radio announced gleefully. What did he care, anyway? He was off work at ten. He could go to the beach and bake in the sun. He could go to Wildwood Park and swim and eat hot dogs and go on a hayride. He could do whatever he wanted to do. Life was so unfair. The rest of America was freezing to death. Why did California always have to be different?

I was so depressed I didn't want to get out of bed. I scrunched up into a tiny ball and concentrated on being the Incredible Shrinking Woman. If I could get small enough, maybe I could disappear. Then the world would forget all about me and I could spend the whole day in bed being miserable.

"Up and at 'em," Dad called on his way down to breakfast. "Too bad you have to work. Your mother's decided the backyard needs a total overhaul. That's what *we* are going to do all day. I'm the 'we' your mother means, of course. What a slave driver. What time are you due at the Holdens?"

"Late, today," I mumbled. I heard him thumping down the stairs without waiting for my answer. He certainly sounded happy for a slave.

Not even getting to drive the car to work made me feel better. What was happening to me? Here I was, a senior, at the high point of my teenage years, and was I having any fun? You better believe I wasn't. I'd taken a job that was supposed to help me get closer to my boyfriend, and because of my job I'd probably lost him altogether. I met another boy. He seemed nice. We became friends. Then, like a jerk, I let him kiss me. Now, instead of being my friend he'd turned on me—and everyone I'd ever known. Almost half my senior year was already gone. The fun, the laughs, the class parties—I was missing it all.

I finally had to get up. But my mood hadn't improved much. Still, for my parents, I put on the "happy face" my dad was always singing about. I even ate my oatmeal wearing a toothpaste-ad grin glued to my face. I helped with the breakfast dishes, kissed Mom and Dad good-bye, then hurried off to my job without the slightest droop of a lip.

The trick was maintaining my false face until I reached the Funny Farm. I was so preoccupied with my miserable lot in life that when I turned onto the Holdens' access road, I forgot all about the dust. I remembered too late. Choking, I pulled over to the side of the road and rolled up the windows.

"You are not going to cry," I warned, digging for a nonexistent tissue in my sweater pocket. "That'll only make things worse." Being covered with dust wasn't my real problem, and I knew it. Missing the swim party was. "You smile," I commanded my face. "You are not going to make Birdie and Noah feel guilty."

It wasn't their fault I'd taken the job they'd offered and it had ruined my whole life. It had been my own decision; I had no one to blame but myself. Lately, it seemed, I was always blaming myself for something. The sad part was, everything probably was my fault!

A tear slipped from the corner of each eye. I wiped them away, leaving a big dirt smudge on my sweater sleeve.

As usual, Birdie was rushing like mad when I arrived at the house. She apologized ten or fifteen different times for having to make me miss the swim party.

Ten or fifteen different times, I said it didn't matter. By the sixteenth "I don't mind. Really. . . ." my "happy face" must have convinced her. Birdie finally left the ranch with Noah without mentioning the party again.

"Well, Sammy," I said, hoisting him onto my hip and carrying him to the family room. "What kind of trouble are you going to get into today?" I put him down on his red tricycle.

He immediately got off and crawled up on the couch.

I sat beside him.

He glared at me from the corner of his eye. Obviously, that was not where he wanted me to sit.

He scampered across the back of the couch and stood poised on the far arm, threatening a death-defying triple-dip dive and back flip combination, landing on his feet (so far I'd been lucky) in the middle of the braided carpet. He pulled his lips back, exposing a mouthful of teeth and gums in that revolting chimp grin he makes and dared me to try and stop him.

I could just hear his little brain clicking away. If I leaped for him, he'd spring into action before I had a hand on him. If I did nothing he might jump anyway. But then again, he might not. I decided to take my chances and opt for "then again, he might not."

"I'm going into the kitchen to see what I can make for our lunch. I don't care if Sammy Holden breaks his little neck," I sang gaily. "Good-bye, Sammy. Have a nice dive." I walked to the kitchen slowly, as if I had nothing to do and all the time in the world to do it in.

It worked. There was no point in trying to annoy me if I wasn't there to notice. Sammy lost interest and followed me to the refrigerator.

I opened the door.

We peered inside together.

"What do you think? How would you like a tuna sandwich made with mayonnaise and onions and a drop of relish, a strawberry cola, barbecued potato chips, and a big slice of your mama's homemade chocolate cake?"

Chattering happily, Sammy grabbed my hand and bounced into the air. He let go and did a somersault.

"Sounds good to me, too." I took the veggies that Sammy would actually get for his lunch from the container marked with his name, and began to clean and cut up raw broccoli. I could make myself the tuna sandwich after he went down for his nap. Sammy would only get the things Birdie had told me to give him.

Sammy waddled over to his private pot cupboard and sat down on the floor in front of the doors. His chattering grew insistent.

"All right. You don't have to shout. You could ask me to open it nicely, instead of shrieking at me." I untied the cord binding the knobs and opened his play cupboard, then I returned to the sink and Sammy's veggies.

Sammy clattered, clashed, and banged with the old pots Birdie had provided to keep him occupied when she had work to do in the kitchen. I watched him from the corner of my eye as I cut up carrots, cauliflower, and celery. He played and I worked and we shouted gibberish to one another over the din.

I made myself stay too busy to dwell on the passing of time. I tried not to think about the swim party that would be starting soon. Or that after the swimming, someone would light the fires in the barbecue pits and they'd drag out the hot dogs and wait for it to get dark (and romantic). And that by then, everyone would have changed out of their swimsuits and dressed in warmer clothes for the eating and the hayride afterward. Only a real nut, I assured myself, would stay in a damp silver bikini all night—especially on a hayride.

I gave up on the "I'm not thinking about anything" game as I fed Sammy his lunch. I'd run out of interesting gibberish to exchange with him before his meal even began. By the time the third handful of carrot-and-broccoli chunks landed in my lap, I'd run out of patience, too. I pulled him out of his seat and carried him to the sink to clean him up. I tried to intimidate him into cooperating by giving him my most frightening glare.

He couldn't have been less impressed. While I was wiping his right hand, his left turned on the water spigot full force, dousing us and the kitchen floor.

I yanked him off the kitchen counter and stomped to the back of the house to change his wet clothes.

"You are going to bed," I announced. "And I am going to . . . cry." That startling revelation was unnecessary. I was already crying.

I was wrong about Sammy going to bed. He had no intention of going to sleep and wasting a perfectly good afternoon of harassing me. Chimpanzees are as smart as people—maybe even smarter. I'd made the fatal mistake of letting him see how preoccupied and vulnerable I was.

Sammy shrieked, and moaned, and battered the sides of his crib, moving it around the room and banging it into his furniture and the bedroom walls. My little cousin could never have kept it up as long as Sammy did. I had no choice but to take him out of bed before he collapsed it, and everything else in his room, too.

I quickly dressed him and put on his jacket with the fleecy

hood. Then I hooked him into his harness and attached his leash. I carried him to his stroller and I jammed him in. We were going out. I was going to push him around the front yard. I hoped the fresh air would tire him out. I was exhausted!

I walked in a circle, pushing the stroller along the uneven path that led around the house. On my third lap I decided to walk along the access road instead. I hoped walking in the dappled sunlight under the trees might not be so boring. I went past my car parked in the driveway and through the yard gate.

Sammy seemed satisfied as long as we kept moving. If I stopped, even for a moment, to admire a plant or watch a bug, he started complaining again. So we kept going, getting farther and farther from the house. We were almost to the end of the dirt road, where it paralleled the street, before Sammy let me slow down.

I was busy watching for ruts in the road, so I wasn't paying too much attention to the street traffic several feet away on the other side of the Holdens' split-rail fence. I didn't realize the truck had stopped until Jon called to me.

"What are you doing down here with Sammy?" he shouted from the truck's open window.

"Walking," I answered curtly. I tried not to look into the truck but my gaze was drawn to the window. I couldn't make out Jon's face inside the cab, it was in the shadows. I knew I was disappointed. I started pushing the stroller again.

"You had better go back," he yelled, allowing the truck to roll along at my pace on the other side of the fence.

"Go away, Jon. I don't need you to tell me what to do."

"You shouldn't have Sammy down here, so close to the main street. It's dangerous."

Sammy had heard Jon's voice and, as usual, had begun a racket of chatters and chirps.

"Thank you for your advice. But lately you seem just a little too free with it. Why don't you wait until someone asks you." I pushed the stroller a little faster, ignoring Sammy's complaints to stop and chat with Jon.

"Sammy can't be trusted, Freddie. He isn't safe around cars. Take him back to the house," he called, as he slowly drove the truck forward.

"Sammy is just fine. I have him in his harness. He's strapped into the stroller. He can't get away." I was practically running now, and I had to shout. I wanted to shout at Jon, I was so angry at him.

"Look, Freddie. I'm sorry you think I'm too free with my advice, but Sammy—"

I cut him off in midstream and turned the stroller around to head back to the house. Not because Jon wanted me to, but because we'd run out of dirt road and were at the main gate.

Jon turned in and pulled the truck up across the lane from Sammy and me. "I'll drive you back to the house," he offered.

"We'll walk," I said and pushed even faster.

I heard the truck gears grind and mesh and the tires grab as it pulled away, but I didn't look up. When I did, all I saw was a battered tailgate in a cloud of dust.

"Who asked you!" I screamed into the swirling mist. "Who asked you anything!" I wiped my eyes on my much used, no longer pink, sweater sleeve.

If I'm going to keep crying all the time, I'm going to have to carry some tissues, I decided, looking down at the dirty brown blotches. If my sweater looked this bad, what did my face look like? I wondered. Probably a smeared-up mess.

"Well, it just so happens that I'm through doing nothing but crying. It's time I did something—even if it's wrong. I'm tired of everybody telling me what I should do, and where I should go, and what I should think. I'm going to do and go and think what I want to, from now on. Do you hear that, Sammy Holden, you little ape?''

Hearing his name took Sammy's attention off the disappearing truck. The chimp spun around in his seat to stare at me. My dirty face or red eyes or something must have looked very funny to him; he gave me a loud chimp laugh. Then he went into his happy act, bouncing up and down on his seat and banging enthusiastically on his stroller tray.

By the time we reached the house, I'd already decided what had to be done. The plan that had formed in my head as I'd marched determinedly up the road was quickly put into action. I didn't waste time on reconsiderations. I was going to do what I had to do. I was going to Wildwood Park to see Darren. I was going to prove to him that I wanted to be his girl.

Taking Sammy's car seat, I carried him, and it, out to my parents' station wagon. I set up the car seat next to me on the passenger's side. Then I very carefully hooked Sammy's leash and halter onto it.

''You see, Sammy, it's like I told that know-it-all, Jonathan Prince. You're perfectly safe when you're all tied in with your halter and leash.''

I started the engine and backed the car out of the Holdens' driveway.

Chapter Fourteen

ONE OF THE BIG problems of living in sunny California, I discovered after we'd moved here, was space. There was too much of the wide-open variety, and not enough of the parking variety. Wildwood Park on a Sunday afternoon was a prime example. The two parking lots closest to the senior swim party were jam-packed with cars. I drove in and out of three more lots before I finally found a space on the far side of the park. I pulled in under a droopy tree and turned off the engine. The lot I was in was very close to the kiddie playground and about as far away as I could get from the area where the senior swim party was happening.

"At least the tree hides the car a little," I muttered, remembering my passenger.

Sammy was asleep in his car seat. His not taking his nap had turned out to be a lucky break for me, after all.

I watched him sleep. His little chest rose and fell rhythmically with each contented breath. Like most babies, he looked like an adorable angel when he was asleep. And like most babies that was the only time he was one. But right now sound asleep was exactly the way I wanted him, so I did everything as quickly and as quietly as I possibly could. I went extra slow and was extra careful so I wouldn't wake him.

I leaned over to check his harness and leash. Before I took one step, I had to know for sure that he was securely fastened into his car seat. I felt each of the rings and clips. Everything was hooked up tight. Sammy wouldn't be going anywhere while I was gone. I rolled down my window about an inch, then I leaned across Sammy and did the same on his side, too. Next, I did something my Aunt Mimmie always does to keep my little cousin Davie from opening the car doors. I wiggled the door handles gently, just to be sure the doors were locked, then I unscrewed all the lock buttons and put them into my sweater pocket with the car keys. I double-checked everything one more time before easing open my door and getting out. I shut my door quietly and locked it from the outside with my key.

Then I walked around the car to see if Sammy looked like a chimp asleep in a car seat or a baby asleep in a car seat. I could barely tell what he was. He was almost invisible under the hanging branches of the weeping willow. Satisfied he would be all right for the ten minutes I needed to get to Darren and bring him back to the car, I jogged away from the parking lot.

My spirits began to fly as I ran toward the area where the swim party was going on. The nearer I got to the sounds of the kids really enjoying themselves, the happier and more optimistic I became.

The hardest part was running past the barbecue pits. The delicious smell of roasting hot dogs made my mouth water and my stomach remembered that, thanks to Sammy, I'd missed lunch.

Kids from school were everywhere. They shouted friendly greetings to me as I ran past. I called and waved without stopping to talk.

It took me a few minutes to find Darren.

He and Sandi were sprawled side by side on a blanket under a large oak tree. Darren's face seemed buried in Sandi's neck. They could have been talking. Or they could have been doing something else.

The red-orange sunlight glittered on Sandi's tiny silver Band-Aids. I'd been wrong. There was at least one person in the world who was crazy enough to sit around in a wet bikini all night.

"Freddie!" Darren shouted and quickly sat up.

Sandi sat up, too, but didn't say anything. She just glared at me.

"What are you doing here?" Darren moved away from Sandi and stood up.

"I came to talk to you, Darren."

"You did? What about—your job? And that monkey?"

"Sammy's an ape," I reminded him.

"Well, I hope you didn't bring that horrible monkey, or whatever it is, with you," said Sandi. Her face wrinkled up in distaste.

"As a matter of fact, I did. Sammy's asleep in the car."

"He must be lonely all by himself—you should go back to him," Sandi said snidely. She leaned back on her elbows and gave Darren and me a clearer view of the scraps of material that made up her sparkling silver attire.

"Speaking of cold, Sandi, aren't you freezing to death in that wet suit? It's almost dark out. Shouldn't you put some warmer clothes on?" I hated the way I sounded—just like her.

"It's not wet. I didn't go in the water. Did we, Darry? And I was just going to change. Can I have the keys to your car?"

Sandi draped herself over Darren's shoulder. "I'll get my clothes, Darry, and be right back."

Darren handed her his keys and she wiggled off toward the parking lot.

"Mason had to come early, so I brought Sandi," he quickly explained. "That's why her clothes . . . I mean, if you're going to get mad or something . . . I just wanted you to know."

"You don't have to explain, Darren. I didn't come here to fight with you—or Sandi. I came to talk to you. Will you come back to my car with me?"

"What's wrong with talking right here? The parking lot's only over there." He pointed in the direction Sandi had taken to get her clothes.

"I'm not in that lot. There weren't any spaces. I'm over there." I pointed in the opposite direction. "By the playground with the little kids' swings and slides."

"Way over there? But the party's just getting good. Let's stay here and talk." Darren sat down on the blanket and patted the space next to him. Then he lay back and put his arms under his head and grinned up at me. "Lie down for a minute, Freddie. It's very comfortable. This can be a very cozy talk we're going to have." He blew me a kiss.

I wanted to. It took all my willpower to shake my head. He looked gorgeous, lying back on the blanket, the glow of the late-afternoon sun glinting off his dark hair. I wanted to say yes, but I knew I couldn't.

"Darren, please stop teasing. I can't stay here. I have to get back to the car. I don't want to leave Sammy alone for too long. Come with me. Please."

He reached out his hand to me.

I thought he wanted me to pull him up. I took his hand and tugged.

He gave my hand a yank and pulled me off-balance. I
landed on the blanket beside him.

"You see. Isn't this much better?" He ran his lips along
the sensitive skin on the inside of my elbow. "You taste
salty," he said, trying to be romantic.

"It's probably sweat. I was running." I was not in a
romantic mood. I'd been away from the car too long. I was
worried about Sammy. Even with all the precautions I'd
taken to be sure Sammy would be safe in the car, I knew I'd
made a big mistake in bringing him with me to the park. I
tried to pull away from Darren. I was beginning to think I'd
been wrong to come at all.

"What's the matter with you? What do you want, anyway?
I didn't ask you to come here looking for me. You came all by
yourself, remember? If you don't like the Gresham
technique, Freddie, vacate the blanket. Someone else will
take your place." He let go of my arm and sat up.

Pulling away from him had hurt his feelings. I was finally
beginning to understand Darren—and his ego. My not re-
sponding to his romantic efforts had wounded his pride. He
had an image (or so he thought) that he had to maintain.
Darren Gresham: Senior Council vice-president, lady-killer
and basketball star. And I'd been the number one member in
his fan club. Now, by not being around, I'd undermined his
confidence, and, in his eyes, his importance.

If I was only one of the numerous members of Darren's
vast fan club, I didn't want to belong at all. Maybe there was
already a new replacement (or several) lined up to take my
place. Maybe it wasn't Sandi Moses, after all. Either way, I
had to know if Darren was using me or if he really cared. Was
I wasting my time even trying to work things out between us?

"Will you come to my car with me or not, Darren? We
need to talk, and I can't stay away any longer."

"Okay. But I want to get back before the hayride." He got to his feet and helped me up. "And I was just going to eat."

Darren came with me reluctantly. He practically dragged his feet like a sullen child. He walked beside me in silence, not even touching my hand. For the first time since we'd started dating, being alone with Darren was making me self-conscious and uncomfortable.

After what seemed like hours, I couldn't stand it anymore. I had to say something. "We're almost there. I left my car just over that little hill."

"What's all the shouting about?" he asked.

"I don't know. Probably a bunch of kids having a birthday party at the playground. Little kids can get pretty rowdy."

"I guess." Darren shrugged. "Sounds more like a circus than a kid's birthday party."

Darren was right—it did.

We ran to the top of the hill. At the bottom, caught in the spotlight of the late-afternoon sun, was the cause of the yelling and shouting. It was a circus. A three-ring circus, with Sammy in the center ring.

I forgot about Darren, I forgot everything, as I ran down the hill toward the swings. "Sammy!" I screamed. "You come down from there this instant. Sammy!"

He was having too good a time being the main attraction to listen to me.

I ran through the exuberantly cheering group of children, shouting at Sammy to no avail. My voice was lost in the shrieks of pure joy from the delighted little half-pints cheering Sammy on.

Their mothers were a different story. A chimp on the loose terrified them. Women screamed and tried to drag their reluctant children away from the wild beast that was now swinging from the top bar of the swing set.

"Monkey! Monkey! Monkey!" shouted the children glee-fully.

Gorilla! Gorilla! Gorilla! said their mothers' faces.

Sammy sprinted across the top of the swing set bar, slid down a leg on the far side, and made for the jungle gym.

"Help me, Darren. He's coming your way. Grab him!" I called.

Darren just stood there like a marble statue. He didn't move. Hs eyes were wide open and glazed like somebody who's been hypnotized. Darren's face said it all: he was really scared of Sammy.

Sammy seemed to sense that Darren was more afraid of him than any of the screaming mothers had been. He scampered up to him, not much higher than Darren's kneecaps, puckered his lips, and let loose the loudest, wettest raspberry. Then the little imp leaned forward on his knuckles and gave Darren the ugliest grin he'd ever made.

Darren stepped back several paces.

Sammy reached out and began to tug on the laces of Darren's tennis shoes. He stuck the end of one in his mouth and started to chew.

Darren jumped.

Sammy complained at the loss of the lace with a loud shriek, then he was off again, scaling the outside of the jungle gym bars.

There was no time to worry about Darren. He'd just have to take care of himself. I went in hot pursuit of my wayward charge.

"Freddie! Stop!"

"Jon!" I stopped short and we collided. "What are you doing here? How did you know? How did you find us?"

"Lucky, I guess. I'll explain later. Would you like a little help catching Sammy?"

"Would I!" I grabbed his hand. "Would I ever."

"Sure she does, Tarzan." Darren suddenly appeared beside me. "You've arrived just in the nick of time. How nice of you to come to the rescue of poor little Jane and her ape."

"Darren!" I'd forgotten all about him. I guess I had just assumed he'd take off and keep going until he got back to Sandi. "Don't call Sammy—or Jon—names, Darren. Sammy didn't do anything to you."

"Only because I didn't give him the chance this time. No hairy little beast's going to bite me and give me rabies."

"If you're so afraid of him, you should have run when you had the chance," Jon pointed out.

For once, I agreed with Jon.

"I'm not afraid of that ugly monkey. What's more, I've had as much of him as I intend to take. This is going to come as a big surprise to you, Freddie, but I've had it with your Jane of Jungleland routine, too. I've had enough of you, and Tarzan, here, and that disgusting miniature King Kong you baby-sit to last a lifetime."

"You watch your mouth, Gresham. You have no right to talk to Freddie like that."

I stared at Jon, speechless. He was defending me. He must not have thought I was a completely worthless social butterfly after all.

"Oh, excuse me. I forgot that Tarzan the Grinder was really Tarzan the Prince. Prince Charming, that is. Well, Prince old man, you have just won yourself the booby prize. You get Jane." Darren turned and quickly walked away.

"Thanks," Jon called after him.

Then Darren spun around and looked right at me. "And Jane—you lose, too. You get to keep King Kong and Prince Charming."

"For your information, Darren Gresham: *I love King Kong*!" I shouted at his retreating back.

The Prince was another story. I wasn't sure how I felt about him.

Chapter Fifteen

KING KONG. . . . How dare Darren call Sammy that!

"Sammy! Oh, no! Jon, look. He's climbing up the rocket ship slide. Oh, please help me catch him before he gets hurt."

"Go to the bottom of the slide. I'll go up after him. I can get him. Don't worry."

Jon gripped one of the tall support poles with his hands, then he wrapped his legs around it. Using the rubber soles of his tennis shoes as a grip for added leverage, he started climbing upward. He wasn't as agile as Sammy, but he kept going.

I ran to the end of the long metal slide and waited. I strained my eyes to watch Jon as he moved up the pole. As the last rays of the day's sun hit him, he seemed to blend in with the fading light. I had to squint to see his grayish-black silhouette dimly outlined against a waning reddish-orange sky.

"Sammy! Where is he, Jon? I can't see him. He's disappeared."

"He swung over to the next pole. I'm going after him."

"Be careful, Jon. Don't fall." Shouldn't I have been thinking of Sammy's safety? I wasn't.

For a moment, Jon seemed suspended in midair as he leaned away from the pole he was on and reached out with his free hand for the next. Then Jon, too, disappeared around the back side of the huge rocket ship. I could hear him trying to soothe Sammy. Jon cooed and coaxed and promised he wasn't mad at him. He tried everything to cajole the chimp into coming closer.

"Yeow!"

I left my post at the bottom of the slide and ran around behind the rocket. "What happened? Are you all right?"

"I made a grab for him and I slipped a little, but I'm fine. Sammy's inside the rocket. Go back and watch the slide. I think we have him now."

"Come down, Jon. Use the ladder to get up into the rocket."

"No. This way is better. You can watch the ladder and the slide. He might come down this pole while I'm climbing up the ladder. I'll be okay. *Go!*"

I went quickly. I watched and I waited.

It had gotten eerily quiet all around me. Only the hum of evening insects disturbed the sudden silence. The shouting and cheering had stopped. Kids and mothers alike were holding their breath, waiting to see what would happen next.

Sammy climbed out of the slide opening in the rocket front and began to scale the nose cone.

Jon appeared in the opening. He started after Sammy. Grasping a crossbar, he hoisted himself off the platform. Then, suddenly, he lost his grip and slipped, dangling precariously by only one hand.

The air came out of all the onlookers at once. We were like

one body with a dozen heads and only one hope—that the boy
and the little chimp got down safely.

Jon reached upward with his free hand, and finding his
hand hold, he pulled himself up.

"Ahhh," we all sighed in unison.

I strained to see through falling darkness. Jon and Sammy
were becoming only a dull blur.

"I've got him. I've got his leash. I'm reeling him in," Jon
called from the top of the nose cone. "Here we come."

Then I could just make them out as they came around to the
front of the nose cone. I wanted to shout with joy as Jon
slowly eased himself down, coming to rest on the rocket
ship's platform. They were both safe.

I could see Jon clearly now, with Sammy clinging to his
neck and chattering away to his best buddy, as if he hadn't a
care in the world. They were so dirty and disheveled. Their
clothes were a mess. Sammy had his harness half on and half
off. They were both a sight—the best sight I'd seen all day.

Jon lowered himself to a sitting position and, holding
Sammy securely in his arms, slid down the slide, landing
with a thump on the ground at my feet.

"Some slide watcher you are, Freddie Larson. Your job
was to stand at the bottom of this thing and catch us. You
were supposed to stop me, not let me fall on my rear end. I
was never any good on a slide." He stood up, handed Sammy
to me, and proceeded to brush himself off.

"Yea! Hurray!" cried the children.

"Thank goodness," said their mothers, their eyes filled
with admiration for Jon.

I just sighed and breathed a little easier. My worries
weren't over yet.

Then, as if the mothers suddenly remembered it was a
chimpanzee they'd been rooting for, every one of them took a

look at Sammy, grabbed up their kids, and headed for the parking lot as fast as they could get away.

Jon walked Sammy and me to my car. We didn't speak. Sammy made enough noise for the three of us.

We stood beside my car for a long minute. Everyone else seemed to have just disappeared, swallowed up by the darkness. Now, except for the three of us—Sammy, Jon, and myself—the parking lot was empty. The sudden stillness was awesome. Even Sammy sat quietly in my arms and listened. There were a few lights scattered around the parking lot. Everywhere else it was dark and strangely quiet.

I shuddered from a sudden chill.

"I think I should drive you and Sammy back to the ranch, now. I'll leave the truck here and come back for it later. You look beat. Both of you." Jon walked the few feet to where he'd parked the truck and locked the doors.

Sammy was tired. He laid his head down on my shoulder and tucked the collar of my knit shirt into his mouth. His soft little sucking sounds were comforting.

"I can drive, Jon. You don't have to make two trips."

"I don't mind. I don't think Sammy would like to be put in a car seat right now. I think what he really needs is to be hugged. Where are your keys?"

I nodded my head. "Right pocket."

Jon took them, then helped Sammy and me into the car. To make room, he put the car seat into the back of the wagon. Then he got in behind the wheel and started the motor.

As we drove out of the lot it all hit me at once. The tiredness, the worry, the guilt, and the shame of what I'd done. In fact, I was so ashamed of myself I was afraid to talk to Jon. I was afraid to hear what he had to say. And when we arrived at the ranch . . . I dreaded that most of all. I would have to face Birdie and Noah. I would have to tell them what I did. How could they ever forgive me? How would I ever forgive myself?

What if they were home already? It was so late, they had to be home. They would be so worried and so scared. I could picture Birdie's frightened face, all white and drawn. I'd caused so much trouble. They had to be worried to death wondering where Sammy and I were. What had I done? And why? No reason I could think of seemed good enough to me now.

The tears slipped down my cheeks before I could stop them. Desperately, I tried to cry without making any noise. I didn't dare wipe away one salty drop; that might draw Jon's attention and I didn't want him to look at me. I didn't want to face the contempt I knew I would find in his eyes.

"You want to talk about it?" he asked.

I stared straight ahead into the glaring flashes of the oncoming headlights and took deep breaths. Did I? Could I talk about what I'd done? With Jonathan Prince?

"Is Sammy asleep?"

I rubbed Sammy's back softly and felt his steady breathing. "Yes."

"That's good. He had quite a time, didn't he?"

"Yes."

"I'll bet all those little kids won't forget today too soon. That was some show Sammy put on."

Neither would I. It would take me a lifetime to forget it. "Jon?"

"What, Freddie?"

"I do want to talk about what happened. I don't expect you to understand why I did what I did, or forgive me; but I would like to try and explain it."

"Okay."

"I was a jerk."

Jon laughed. "That explains it."

"Jon, please. I'm serious. You were right about me and my friends. Except Barbara and Wiz—they're great. But Darren, Sandi, Mason, Janet, Richard, and especially me, we're all sad cases. Empty-headed social butterflies just like you said. The thing is . . . I didn't have to be. It was my own choice. And I chose to put having a boyfriend and a fun senior year before my responsibilities and obligations. Responsibilities and obligations I didn't have to have. I took them on myself."

"Look, Freddie. I do understand."

"I don't see how you could. You'd never do the terrible thing I did. You don't let people down, Jon. You didn't let me down today, did you?"

"I'm no saint, Freddie. I didn't come after you just because of Sammy."

"Why did you come, Jon? How did you know where to find me?"

"Finding you was easy—sort of. I went over to where the senior party was and asked Sandi where you and Darren were. She pointed in this direction, and I just drove in and out of every parking lot until I found your car."

"But how did you know I'd taken Sammy and we'd gone to the senior party?"

"I came by the house to apologize for what I said the other day. I guess I just wanted to talk. You and Sammy weren't there. I knew how much you wanted to be at the swim party. Remember, you told me you asked Birdie for the day off. And she told me how bad she felt turning you down. And, since I knew how much you thought you loved Darren Gresham, I just put it all together and bingo—right on target."

"I don't know why I did something so stupid."

"Because you were in love?"

"No. I wasn't in love, Jon. I was infatuated with good times and popularity. Just like you told me. Heaven only knows what could have happened to Sammy today. All because I wanted to be a part of the 'in' crowd.''

"Aren't you being a little tough on yourself?''

"Not tough enough. I just can't imagine how Sammy got loose. I had him harnessed into his car seat and his leash was hooked up and the doors were all locked. . . .''

"He unhooked himself. I tried to tell you that this morning. Just because you have him hooked in, that doesn't mean you're home safe. You've heard of Harry Houdini? This chimp is his brother, Hairy Holdini. I'm surprised Noah didn't warn you about him. Sammy's a professional escape artist. That's one of the reasons he needs a sitter. There isn't a jail that can hold him.''

I surprised myself by laughing.

"Oh. And by the way . . . he's also real good at rolling car windows up and down.''

"I noticed.'' I hugged Sammy a little closer.

I was so lucky to have him back safe and sound. Whatever the Holdens did to me, I had it coming. I was just grateful that Sammy didn't have to suffer for my stupidity. I really did love my little King Kong.

Suddenly, I was crying again. This time with relief.

"Don't do that, Freddie.'' Jon's arm was around my shoulder, pulling me as close to him as my seat belt would allow. "Please don't cry. Everything will be all right. You'll see. You don't need Darren and his crowd. You're a special person without them.''

"I am?'' My head leaned against his shoulder and I let it stay there.

"To me you are.'' His fingers touched my cheek. He moved his hand across my shoulder and patted Sammy gently. Then, very softly, he began to stroke my arm.

The closer we got to the Funny Farm, the more painful my breathing got, and the more my stomach gurgled and churned. I didn't try to tell Jon it wasn't Darren or his "in" crowd I was worried about. They no longer mattered to me at all. All I really cared about was what the Holdens thought of me—and what Jon thought of me—and what I was thinking about myself.

I guess I didn't realize there was one other opinion that counted to me, too. One I'd forgotten all about.

"This is it," Jon said, as we turned off the main street and onto the dirt access road leading to the ranch house.

"This" felt like the stuff tornadoes were made of. My insides did a nose dive into my tennis shoes.

Jon patted my shoulder reassuringly. "They're waiting for us," he said, pointing toward Birdie and Noah standing on the front porch.

I swallowed hard.

"Sammy! Oh, Sammy!" shouted Birdie. She hurried down the porch steps and was running toward the car before Jon had the motor off.

"Is everything okay?" Noah asked when he reached the car. His question was directed at Jon, who was already getting out on his side.

Jon nodded his head. "Everything is fine, Noah."

Birdie pulled opened my door and took Sammy from my arms.

Sammy stirred and opened his eyes. If chimps can really smile, I think he did when he saw his mommy.

"Where were you, sweet thing? Mommy was so worried," Birdie cooed and snuggled Sammy.

He was silent.

Noah was silent.

Jon was silent.

Now, even Birdie was silent.

Everybody looked at me.

"I'm so sorry, Birdie—Noah. I'm so very sorry." I fought the tears that threatened to overwhelm me. I wasn't going to get hysterical as a bid for forgiveness. I didn't deserve sympathy.

"Sorry? For what, Freddie?" Noah asked.

"For taking Sammy away from the ranch without your permission." As terrified as I was, I had to tell it all. There couldn't be any half-truths now.

"Why would you do that?" asked Noah.

"I took him to the park where my class party was being held. Then I did a really dumb thing. I left him alone in the car . . . not for long, though. Honest. I thought he was all strapped in, safe and sound, but he got out. He unhooked his harness and rolled down the window. I didn't even know he could do that. But nothing happened. I swear it. Sammy just put on a little show for some small children on the kiddie playground apparatus. Then Jon came and he helped me catch Sammy and bring him home."

"You went to the senior party, too, Jon?" Birdie asked him. Her voice held disbelief.

"No. He didn't. He came after me. He knew what I had done was stupid and that I'd probably need help. Don't be mad at Jon. He didn't do anything wrong. I did. I did it all. If anything had happened, it would have been all my fault. Jon was wonderful. Really he was."

Birdie hugged Sammy to her. Both she and Noah smiled warmly at Jon. They didn't blame him.

"I don't know what to say." Noah sighed deeply. "We trusted you, Freddie."

"We left our baby in your care," Birdie added.

"I know. There is nothing I can say to make up for what I've done. But . . . please let me try."

"How? How can you?" Birdie demanded.

"By continuing to sit for Sammy. By being the very best sitter in the whole world."

Noah looked at me long and hard. "You're asking us to take a chance with Sammy; he's like our child. A second chance, Freddie. That's a lot to ask. We love Sammy."

"I love Sammy, too."

"She does, Noah. I believe her, Birdie." Jon was defending me again. His confidence and support meant everything to me.

"I don't know. . . ." Noah looked at me. He looked at Birdie.

She looked concerned and confused. She shifted the yawning Sammy to her other arm. Birdie studied me with soft brown eyes I couldn't read.

Sammy looked at me, too. He pulled back his lips in his ugly chimp grin and chattered happily. Then he put out his arms to me.

I put my arms out to him, too.

Sammy came to me, chirping and hugging and kissing me.

I kissed him back.

He cuddled into my arms and settled down to finish sucking the life out of my shirt collar.

Birdie and Noah laughed.

"Obviously, Sammy wants you to have that second chance," said Noah.

"He loves you, too, Freddie," Birdie said. "I think he's right. Sammy's a very good judge of character."

I remembered Sammy's reaction to Darren. He *was* a good judge of character. A much better one than I was.

"Thank you, Sammy Holden." I kissed the top of his head.

"You better give him to me," said Birdie. "I think it's time this little rascal had some dinner and said good night. Come to Mommy, sweetheart." Birdie reached for Sammy, but instead gathered us both up into her arms and hugged Sammy and me together. Then she kissed my cheek.

"Thank you, Birdie," I whispered.

"Thank you, too, Freddie. For loving our Sammy." She took Sammy from me and carried him into the house.

"Well," Noah said. "I guess I'll leave you two to figure out how you're going to get home." He winked at Jon.

Jon smiled. And, although the porch light in front of the ranch house was dim, I think he blushed.

"I'll get the truck tomorrow, Noah," said Jon. "My mom can drive me over to the park on my way to work. That is, if Freddie will drop me at home tonight?"

I nodded. My parents would certainly lend me the car a little bit longer. Taking Jon home was definitely one of those emergencies they'd promised I could use it for.

"Good night, you two," said Noah.

"Good night," Jon and I said together.

"And thank you," I added.

We watched Noah go into the house and close the door.

"Shall I drive?" I asked Jon.

"No. I like to drive my girls around."

His girl? Is that what he thought? Well, the idea wasn't all that distasteful. I'd think about it.

Jon walked me to the passenger's side and opened the door.

I started to get in.

He put his hand on my arm and stopped me. "Freddie?"

I straightened up and looked at his smiling face. "Yes, Jon."

"Freddie. I'm glad the way things turned out."

"I am, too, Jon."

"Do you think not being Darren's girl will make a big difference?"

"Yes, I do."

"Oh."

"A wonderful one."

"Oh!" Jon put his arms around my waist.

I let my body lean softly against his. I could feel his warmth as he pulled me closer. My ear was so close to his heart that its beating vibrated into me and my heart joined his in rhythm. I took deep breaths and tried to keep my knees from buckling underneath me.

"Freddie, I'm glad you're not anybody's special girl anymore. At least not for a little while."

"You are?" I asked innocently.

"Do you think a grinder has a chance with one of the prettiest, nicest, most popular girls in our school?"

"Are you willing to take a chance on it, Jon?"

He tightened his grip.

"Do you think an empty-headed social butterfly has a chance with one of the handsomest, brightest, and sweetest guys at school?" I asked.

"You can plan on it," he answered.

Then Jon kissed me.

I'd felt so awful all day. But now, in Jon's arms, I suddenly felt so warm and wonderful inside. I wouldn't have traded places with anyone in the whole wide world. After all, how often does a girl answer a want ad to baby-sit a chimpanzee and find a little love and her very own Prince Charming?